Frozen Sky 2: Betrayed

Jeff Carlson

International bestselling author
of *Plague Year* and *Interrupt*

Jeff Carlson
www.jverse.com

Film / TV
Jim Ehrich
Rothman Brecher Kim Agency
9250 Wilshire Blvd., 4th Fl.
Beverly Hills, CA 90212
310-432-4629

Literary
Don Maass
Donald Maass Literary Agency
121 West 27th St., Ste. 801
New York, NY 10001
212-727-8383

First Edition
ISBN 978-0-9960823-1-0
Copyright © 2014 Jeff Carlson

Cover art by Jasper Schreurs Copyright © 2014

European Space Agency maps and schematics by Jeff Sierzenga. Copyright © 2014. Reproduced with permission.

Other Books
by Jeff Carlson

Interrupt

The Europa Series
The Frozen Sky
Betrayed
Blindsided
Battlefront

The Plague Year Trilogy
Plague Year
Plague War
Plague Zone

Short story collection
Long Eyes

Praise for
The Frozen Sky

"I'm hooked."
—Larry Niven, *New York Times* bestselling author of *Ringworld*

"A first-rate adventure set in one of our solar system's most fascinating places. This is his best book yet."
—Allen Steele, Hugo Award-winning author of the *Coyote* series

"Pulse pounding."
 —*Publishers Weekly*

"Intelligent and entirely new. Highly recommended."
—Seanan McGuire, *New York Times* bestselling author of *Chimes At Midnight*

"Nothing short of amazing."
—David Marusek, Sturgeon Award-winning author of *The Wedding Album*

"Deep and complex. Nail-biting."
—Bookbanter.net

Praise for the
Plague Year trilogy

"An epic of apocalyptic fiction: harrowing, heartfelt, and rock-hard realistic."
 —James Rollins, *New York Times* bestselling author of *Bloodline*

"Chilling and timely."
 —*RT Book Reviews*

"I can't wait for the movie."
—*Sacramento News & Review*

Praise for
Interrupt

"Carlson is dangerous. Thumbs up."
—Scott Sigler, *New York Times* bestselling author of *Pandemic*

"This book has it all — elite military units, classified weaponry, weird science, a dash of romance, and horrific global disasters. Carlson writes like a knife at your throat."
—Bob Mayer, *New York Times* bestselling author of the *Green Berets* and *Area 51* series

"The ideas fly as fast as jets."
—Kim Stanley Robinson, Hugo Award-winning author of *2312*

For Ute and Bill.

Thank you for always
standing by us.

TABLE OF CONTENTS

Timeline

900 through 1200 AD: Chinese alchemists and artillery experts develop "fire arrows," the world's first crude rockets, to repel Mongol invasions.

1200 through 1350 AD: The Mongol Empire adapts fire arrow technology in its conquests of Asia, Russia, and Europe.

1300 through 1800 AD: Cannon and incendiary weapon programs advance throughout the regions exposed to Mongol and Chinese power.

1792: India uses the world's first iron-cased rockets against the British.

1803 through 1815: The British develop cylindrical iron warhead rockets, which they use against French and American forces.

1903: Russian mathematician Konstantin Tsiolkovsky publishes the first detailed work on rocket propulsion for space travel.

September 1944 through March 1945: The German *Wehrmacht* launches thousands of V-2 rockets against British and other Allied targets.

August 6 1945: The United States Of America deploys fission weapons against Japan.

October 4 1957: The Union Of Soviet Socialist Republics launches *Sputnik*, Earth's first orbiting satellite.

The "Golden Age" begins

July 20 1969: Neil Armstrong walks on the moon.

March 1972 and April 1973:   NASA launches unmanned probes *Pioneer 10* and *Pioneer 11*.

November 1973 through December 1974:   *Pioneer* flybys of Jupiter.

August and September 1977: NASA launches unmanned probes *Voyager 1* and *Voyager 2*.

March through July 1979: *Voyager* flybys of Jupiter and Europa.

1981 through 2011:   The USSR and the USA each develop and operate partly reusable low Earth orbit spacecraft.

Beginning 1986:   The USSR and its successor, the Russian Federation, construct and maintain humankind's first space station, *Mir*.

December 1995: NASA unmanned probe *Galileo* reaches Jupiter and performs dozens of orbits and close observations through 2003. When the probe's energy systems begin to fail, NASA deliberately plunges *Galileo* into Jupiter's atmosphere to avoid striking any of its moons and contaminating those environments, three of which hold liquid water.

October 15 1997:   NASA, the ESA and the Italian Space Agency design and launch unmanned probe *Cassini-Hyugens* bound for Saturn.

Beginning 1998:   The United States Of America, the Russian Federation, the ESA, Japan and Canada construct and maintain a larger, more permanent orbital platform called the *International Space Station*.

Late 2000: *Cassini* flybys of Europa.

So-called "Blind Age" begins

March 21 2001: *Mir* burns up in Earth's atmosphere.

September 11 2001: Prominent terrorist attacks in USA.

October 7 2001: USA invades Afghanistan.

March 20 2003: USA invades Iraq.

Beginning 2007: The Long Recession debt crisis. Global economy crashes, then remains suppressed for more than a decade.

July 21 2011: NASA shuttle program discontinued.

October 30 2022: Day One of the November Revolution in the Russian Federation, henceforth known as Great Russia. "Dirty bomb" strikes across eastern Europe. Ecological disasters. Global markets collapse.

February 4 2028: Military coups in Beijing, Hanoi, and Pyŏngyang usher in the formation of the People's Supreme Society Of China.

February 27 2028: Assassination of Premier Kiông in Taiwan.

February 24 2028 through July 1 2035: Brazilian invasions of Paraguay, Columbia, and French Guiana draw USA and EU forces to South America.

September 20 2034: South Korea falls to PSSC Liberation Army.

"New Cold War" begins

January 2037: PSSC launches a next-gen series of reusable space shuttles.

2040 through 2085: PSSC constructs several orbital stations, igniting new tension between the western nations and a far-flung alliance led by PSSC, Brazil, Iran, and Great Russia. Beginning in 2049, the western nations begin constructing their own orbital platforms. Four decades of the renewed Space Race result in limited colonization of the moon and Mars, asteroid mining, and a PSSC deep space probe to Pluto as a show of technological might.

October 14 2094: NASA astronauts land on Europa, establishing mecha teams to process deuterium for the western military and civilian fleets.

December 29 2094: PSSC mecha land on Europa.

March 23 2096: ESA mecha land on Europa.

June 7 2096: The One-Day War. Great Russia devastated. Kinetic missile strikes include London, Paris, Miami, and Nanjing.

June 10 2096: Armistice declared.

November 25 2096: Formation of the Allied Nations.

"Restabilization" begins

October 7 2097: A.N. treaties affirm international law exclusively limiting Near Earth Space, the moon, Mars, and all celestial bodies to non-military purposes.

May 1 2098: PSSC spy sats identify American missile platform in Earth orbit.

May 3 2098: American government publicly shares data on similar missile platforms operated by the PSSC in Earth orbit and above Mars.

May 6 2098: The *Rodgers* Incident — a PSSC cruiser collides with an American shuttle near the suspected missile platform. Six PSSC marines killed. Emergency councils in Geneva and Beijing.

Beginning 2101: PSSC commissions five new *Yinglong*-class destroyers.

January 2 2113: ESA mecha discover primitive lifeforms (deceased) on Europa.

April 20 2113: A three-member international science team leaves Earth orbit aboard the Deep Space Reconnaissance ESA *Marcuse*, a low-gee ship on a long-term mission. They will require eleven weeks to travel to Europa.

June 22 2113: Chinese mecha open a tunnel in the ice lined with what appears to be a "library" of hieroglyphics and biological materials constructed by intelligent alien lifeforms.

June 26 through July 1 2113: New high-gee ships leave Earth orbit.

July 11 2113: ESA *Marcuse* lands on Europa.

July 13 2113: Bauman, Vonderach and Lam enter the tunnel, setting off a cave-in. Bauman and Lam are killed. Vonderach is trapped beneath the ice.

July 15 2113: First Contact.

July 16 through July 23 2113: High-gee ships from the PSSC, the ESA, NASA, and the FNEE reach Europa.

July 17 2113: Vonderach rescued by NASA mecha.

July 18 through July 24 2113: Exploration / scientific / diplomatic efforts begin. Contact made with v arious sunfish tribes by NASA, the ESA, and the PSSC.

August 2 2113: FNEE military incursion thwarted by ESA cyber attacks.

August 24 2113: Political agreements reached on Earth between the European Union and Brazil. New FNEE incursion supported by ESA mecha. FNEE gun platforms ambush and surround Top Clan Two-Four until another, unknown tribe opens a geyser, causing blowouts on the surface; ESA Astronauts Collinsworth and Pärnits are killed; ESA Hab Module 03 is destroyed along with one hundred and forty-three listening posts, relays, beacons, and other mecha.

August 28 2113: Treaty formed by the ESA and Top Clan Eight-Six.

September 9 2113: ESA Submodule 07 constructed beneath the surface...

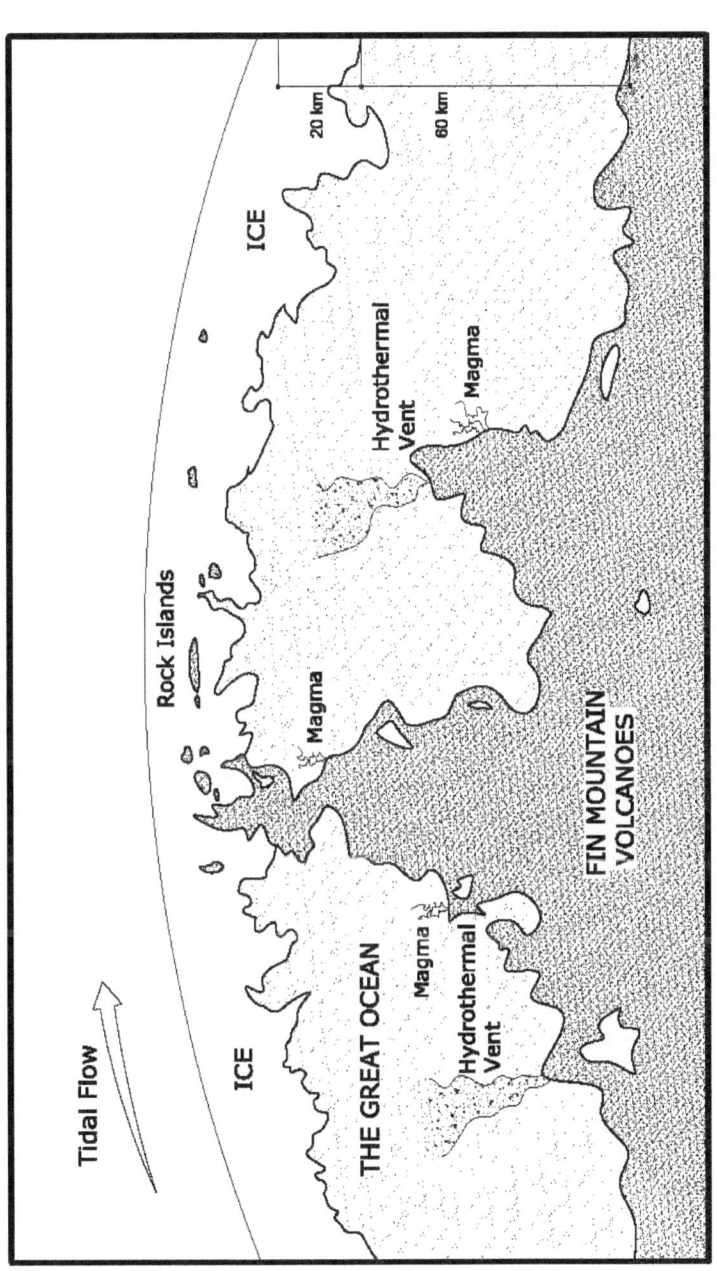

Europa's Southern Pole

BETRAYED

1.

The ice shook again. Vonnie felt a groaning movement through the steel floor of Submodule 07. Every vibration traveled through her bare feet into her legs and spine, invading her bones, rippling through her nerves and flesh.

It scared her. Submodule 07 was ten meters beneath the surface. A thousand tons of ice encompassed her, and she'd darkened the room except for one heads-up display.

The display had shown a stream of alien hieroglyphics. Now it flickered. The eight-armed shapes winked on and off like a living mass of sunfish.

Vonnie tried to stay calm. She was thirty-six years old and had worked for Arianespace or the ESA for a decade, first as an engineer, then as a member of an elite off-world crew. She trusted their sensors. *Ben didn't forecast any quakes. This is just another tremor*, she thought until the module shuddered with two noises like rifle fire — like the insulated hull had ripped apart.

Krakkak!

Red alarms filled her display. Inside, the module was a steel box lined with cabinets and her data/comm station. Outside, struts and mooring cables bristled from the exterior.

Three struts had torn on the west side. The hull was under stress, although if it had split, the fractures were thin since she hadn't experienced decompression. Not yet. But there were other dangers in the ice.

Suddenly the floor dropped. Vonnie's jaw muscles tightened and her posture changed as she spread her arms, struggling for balance. Her tall, lean body bent at the hips.

Behind her in the darkness, a sunfish screeched.

Oh God.

The alien's scream was real, not a simulation like the complicated dance of eight-armed shapes on her display. A living sunfish was inside the module with her. Its beak clacked as it inhaled the oxygen-rich air.

Vonnie turned to fight. She bared her teeth and raised her fists, which were unprotected like her feet. Submodule 07 was as warm as a summer day on Earth. She wore a tank top, shorts, and a med systems bracelet. Her forearm and the bracelet made a poor club. Its nano circuitry weighed a few ounces and its wrist band was soft mesh — but the alumalloy edges of its casing would appear bright and hard to a sunfish.

The alien screeched again, reading Vonnie with its sonar calls. Then it leapt at her.

More than a meter wide, it was a writhing albino monster. The body at its center was a flattened ball ringed with eight tentacles. Blunt dorsal spikes armored its topside. On its underside, its arms were lined with thousands of tube feet and pedicellaria like squirming hair. Gill slits and a sharp, compact beak were the sole features on its belly. No eyes. No nose. No ears except well-protected nubs hidden in the grooves between its arms.

"Come on!" Vonnie yelled.

Deafening the sunfish was her first weapon. Crouching on the floor — taking the low position — was her second.

As the sunfish flew closer, Vonnie pistoned upward to block it, using all of the sinewy muscles in her abdomen and thighs. She knew better than to let it get behind her. At the same time, she swung her right fist up and over in a high roundhouse punch. She wanted to strike its topside. She needed to avoid the grasping, cutting snarls of its pedicellaria. One good blow would stun it. She was stronger than a sunfish. But it was faster.

It curled two of its arms and glommed onto her wrist. Then it clutched at her head with six more arms. It scratched her ears, her collarbone, her temples, her chin.

The floor shuddered again and threw Vonnie sideways. Outside, the ice rumbled.

Impossibly, the sunfish anticipated the complex interaction of the seesawing floor and her jerking body. It scrabbled past her hands, spreading its arms like a hideous flower. It stank. Its breath smelled of feces and carrion.

"Yaaaaaaaah!" Vonnie screamed.

She grabbed one of its gill slits with her right hand, then locked her arm and neck, using her skeleton like a jack to hold the sunfish at bay.

It twisted bonelessly around her. It slithered toward her face. She pummeled its topside with her left fist, but the dry cartilage of its skin felt like rubber. The pedicellaria beneath its arms were an undulating nightmare.

Yanking on her short hair, it dragged her face closer to its snapping beak.

"No! No!"

One of its arms had been severed in its past. The scar-ravaged stump was a weak spot. Vonnie wrestled her shoulder against the amputation. She let the sunfish enfold her right arm. Then she levered it away from her head, barely noticing when it peeled her skin apart.

She slammed the sunfish against the ceiling and roared, "You son of a bitch!"

It screeched at her. Its high-pitched sonar caused an eerie ringing in her skull, but she leaned closer, deliberately exaggerating her grimace.

Its species understood threat displays — and in its culture, the submissive position was above. Standing on the module floor, Vonnie had the dominant position. Her size added to her bid for control.

She yelled again. "Yaaaaah!"

Its arms cinched tighter on her wounds. Blood fell onto her cheek. The hot moisture stung her eyes, yet she refused to lean back. She kept her teeth bared.

I'm hurt, she thought.

Worse, the sunfish was surely tasting her gore through the tube feet mingled among its pedicellaria. Second by second, it was regaining energy, absorbing protein from her with the accelerated metabolism of its race.

Vonnie had fought her battles in an armored suit or standing at a data/comm station. Her species conducted war by mecha, satellites, missiles, and SCPs. To the sunfish, combat was a pheromone-infused spasm of rock clubs, beaks, and cannibalism. Its tolerance for pain and filth far exceeded her own. It would eat from her until her victory was indisputable both physically and mentally.

"Stop!" she yelled. "Don't make me kill you!"

It screeched again.

"Stop!"

Now it shrilled — a plaintive sound? — and Vonnie risked a look over her shoulder to assess the module.

Outside, the ice was settling. She heard a *bang* as a chunk dropped onto the roof, but there were none of the louder noises of an ongoing quake. The tremor was over.

She hadn't lost her air. Was the module intact? The room was lighter now, not red, which meant her display had turned off its alarms. She saw a flurry of reports from the ESA grid. Faintly, she realized she'd also been listening to human voices. The radio was loud but not as loud as her heartbeat or the agony in her arm.

"Von! Von! Talk to me!" Ben shouted as Koebsch said in the background, "Pull her up and warn the tribes. Keep our mecha on alert. We can't—"

"I'm all right!" Vonnie yelled.

"We can't do this again," Koebsch said.

"Don't pull me up. I'm all right." Vonnie kept her face aimed at the sunfish as she spoke. Holding its compact body against the ceiling, she jammed her elbow into its stomach like a bully taking a cheap shot. "Right!?" she yelled.

The sunfish pulled four of its arms from her torn flesh. Then it rustled its body in a clockwise movement, curling each arm tip.

Vonnie recognized the gesture. She relaxed, and her grin

faded. She felt woozy. She needed medical care, but dealing with the sunfish was more important.

She stepped back and let go.

"What are you doing?" Koebsch asked as Ben said, "Von? Are you sure?"

"Yes. It was my fault." Carefully maintaining her assertive tone and posture, Vonnie clamped her left hand on her wounds.

The sunfish stayed above her. It clung to an unilluminated light panel, bunching its arms in rapid patterns as it emitted its sonar calls.

Vonnie nodded in response. From the very beginning, sunfish had understood human physiology well enough to identify the head as the center of their best sensory organs and their primary source of communication. It answered her nod with another clockwise movement of its arms.

"The quake surprised us both, but I acted wrong," Vonnie said. "I showed fear. I showed mistrust."

"You're injured," Koebsch said.

She managed to smile. "It won't be my first skin graft. The AI can handle it."

"Von, he mutilated you! He was chewing on your arm! What if he gets to your eyes next?"

"It wouldn't be my first transplant, either," she said. "Please. Be quiet and let me work."

Koebsch was eleven years older than Vonnie, more conservative, even fatherly since she'd rebuffed his overtures as a potential suitor. His exasperation with her grew into disappointment. "That woman is a lunatic," he announced as if speaking to someone else. Vonnie knew the comment was meant for her and for the virtual presence of leaders in Berlin, Washington, Tokyo and Brasilia.

She smiled again. Nine weeks after First Contact, there were less than sixty people on Jupiter's ice moon Europa, but they were heavily outnumbered by electronic ghosts.

Hundreds of AI proxies had been transmitted from Earth by government bureaucrats, generals, corporate heads and the officials of various space agencies. *Homo sapiens* always tried to install top-down hierarchies. It was their nature. Her rules of engagement were extensive. Everything she did was monitored. Every day the proxies argued with Koebsch, wasting time, wasting energy, while Vonnie and the other astronauts dealt with the situation in real-time. Earth was too far away to interfere effectively.

"Okay," she said. "Okay."

Blood dripped lazily from her arm, slowed by Europa's .13 gravity. She knelt over the red splatter on the floor. Then she gestured with her fingers bent as wide and as far back as possible, an invitation.

"Come on," she said. "It's okay, Tom."

The sunfish was her friend.

2.

Tom leapt down beside her, shrilling. Vonnie's skin prickled at the sensation. Most of the frequencies he used were imperceptible to human ears, a torrent of sound that she felt rather than heard.

Is he reading me from the angles of my skeleton as well as the tension in my voice? she wondered.

On Earth, searching for prey, bats produced ten to twenty clicks per second, a rate that briefly intensified when they located their targets. Moments before killing their prey, bats' sonar calls escalated into a "terminal buzz" of two hundred clicks per second. But they couldn't sustain these screams.

With four air sacs squeezing the same breath back and forth through a corded larynx, sunfish were capable of creating sounds almost without pause. Their talents also went beyond mere echolocation. They used ultra- and infrasound.

Tom could "see" through her. Emitting more than four hundred pulses per second, he screeched again, adjusting many of his cries to wave-lengths that were audible to her. Vonnie recognized the tone. He was questioning her, challenging and probing her.

"We're okay," she said. She extended her bare foot. Tom caressed her ankle, then explored her toes. "I need medical," she said. "You know medical? The machine?"

Tom shrilled again, snarling himself around her leg. Vonnie shivered at his grip, but she did not flinch.

His hellish needs and reflexes were why the ESA biologists had warmed the module. They'd wanted to entice him. Deviously, they'd also planned to calm him. Sunfish loved heat. Within the frozen sky, they fought for warm environments more than they fought for food. Most of the time, Tom grew unusually sluggish as he basked in the high, steady temperature.

Vonnie had decided against wearing armor with the same intent, not because the module was hot, but to soothe Tom. Her fingers and toes were an integral part of talking with him. The sunfish communicated mostly by sonar and touch. Her shape was wrong for their body language, and she could never smell or taste right, yet when she rocked her ankle, Tom nestled closer like a child might respond to a tickle or a hug.

She didn't believe his attack had been meant to kill. Within their tribes, the sunfish were rough on each other. They provoked and intimidated their peers. Their group dynamic was always in flux. Drawing blood during an exchange of ideas or moods was normal — and outside their tribes, they were absolutely savage.

The sunfish were quick to fight, quick to heal, quick in everything except to make peace. They matured quickly and bred quickly. Their lives were short by human standards. After twenty Earth years, a sunfish was elderly, although it was rare for them to reach old age. They also died quickly, either in natural catastrophes like quakes and volcanic eruptions or during their wars with each other.

"Careful now," Vonnie said. Her mild tone was for the benefit of everyone watching her as well as Tom. "Med systems up. Move at half speed. Don't upset him."

"Roger that," Ben said on her display.

The medical AI would operate with more skill than anyone using manual control, so Ben merely confirmed its decisions as it extended two wire probes from the wall. Nevertheless, she appreciated the comfort of his voice.

Ben was closer to her age than Koebsch. He was forty-three, squat and coarse and sweet. He'd been a hothead when they first met. Weeks later, he'd mellowed in some ways. He was less sarcastic with their crewmates and saved his most biting remarks for Koebsch, harassing him. Ben obviously hoped to widen the distance between Vonnie and Koebsch.

Men, she thought with irritation, trying to suppress the pain in her arm. She shouldn't have let her wounds unsettle her. Fidgeting in discomfort, she moved Tom closer to the wire probes. He clacked dangerously. Then his arms cinched on her leg like a knot of heavy snakes.

"Watch it," Ben said.

"Sorry."

"Let me route the probes away from him."

"Thank you, Ben."

Finally, the AI slipped its tools into her flesh, injecting her with trauma meds and nanotech. Vonnie sagged in relief.

"You're gonna have one long sexy scar," Ben said.

Vonnie laughed. The noise evoked a new pattern of stroking from Tom, who recognized the joyful sound. Simultaneously, he screeched at the probes.

Was he jealous of the probes' intimacy with her bleeding arm? Did he feel excluded or threatened?

Vonnie glanced at her display. She'd learned to read Tom with some reliability by herself, but, ironically, she wasn't always certain what *she* was saying, so the AIs did more than transcribe Tom's cries and body language. The AIs also interpreted the totality of her body, voice, and biochemistry as Tom might perceive her.

VONNIE: Wary and hurt / I'm hurt / Determined / I can hurt you if you attack again.

TOM: You taste like fear but you show patience.

VONNIE: We are friends / You hurt me.

TOM: Friends / Fear.

VONNIE: Show patience.

TOM: Don't like your fear / Hate your machines / Hate your homes / Need food and air.

VONNIE: I can protect you from the machines.

TOM: Yes / Protect.

A third probe extended to spray bandages on her arm. Tom's agitation increased. He recoiled, then screeched at the plastic stink.

TOM: Kill it / Hurt you / Kill it.

VONNIE: Patience.

TOM: Hurt you / Make it go.

The third probe was done. It withdrew. "Shhh, Tom," she said. "They're fixing me."

What did she smell like to him? Her gore must have had an inviting aroma. Now her injuries were sealed beneath the spray. Tom had lost the scent of her blood, and new pain flared through her ankle as he squeezed.

Koebsch is right, she thought. *I'm too obsessive.*

Not everyone understood the responsibility she felt to help the sunfish. Fewer shared her commitment. Many people, even highly trained astronauts, had difficulty seeing past their own egos.

Two months ago, the same had been true for Vonnie. She'd forced her way into a tunnel carved with hieroglyphics because she'd wanted to be the first explorer inside Europa. Her wish had come true. The cost had been the lives of two friends and uncounted sunfish. Lost in the ice, she'd left a path of destruction through their colonies. She'd killed dozens of them, so she could accept some risk and pain to settle her debt. The main thing was learning to communicate.

I should have waited to deal with my arm, she realized. *If I was a sunfish, I would have bled until my tribe stopped it by applying pressure. We could have bonded over the taste and scent.*

"Ben, take off my bandages," she said.

"Why the hell would I do that?"

"The nanotech will stop the bleeding," she said. "Take off my bandages."

"There are fractures in your ulna and thumb. If I—"

"Don't use a new probe. Tom is too edgy. The micro clusters in place can do the job."

"Christ. You're going to feel it."

"Not with the meds."

"I warned you," Ben said. He sent new commands to the AI. Then the surgical tools in her arm bulged, opening holes like pores through her bandages.

It didn't hurt. She was numb. But the pressure was abrupt. "Oh!" she cried.

"Are you all right?"

"Oh, fine," she said, modulating her voice like a song as Tom lifted two arms. He'd scented her wounds. His muscular grip eased on her leg and she crooned, "I'm fine. We're fine. It's not bad. Thank you, Ben."

Tom chirped, his pedicellaria rasping on her skin. Was he happy? Restless? Angry?

He feels all three, she thought before she looked at her display. Her instinct was correct. The translation of Tom's behavior showed pleasure mixed with belligerence.

The sunfish never let go of their hostility. Europa was far more unstable than Earth. Their decisions were always for the short term, ready to fight, ready to die, and Vonnie enjoyed the challenge of introducing them to larger things. Her ancestors had been problem-solving apes who'd actively sought new mysteries as they spread from jungles to grasslands to mountains to shores. The sunfish possessed many of the same characteristics. They were clever and nomadic and unique. Vonnie didn't understand people who didn't understand her excitement or the kinship she felt.

We have every advantage over the sunfish, she thought. *Knowledge. Medicine. We can afford to be charitable. What would it say about us if we weren't generous?*

While the probes operated on her arm, she rubbed her left hand on Tom's bumpy topside, increasing her physical contact. As quickly as his species resorted to violence, they were also mollified by the simplest gestures.

If they had fur, she assumed they'd be more popular. They would seem more like dogs or cats — fuzzy little inferior creatures who were easy to manipulate. Instead, millions of people regarded the sunfish with horror. Many said humankind should leave Europa and abandon the tribes to their dying world. But they were sentient. Once upon a time, they'd created an empire within the ice before it was destroyed by volcanic upheavals. They were capable of philosophy and laws.

Yes, they were vicious. She'd been forced to kill them in self-defense. The sunfish had swarmed her. First she'd crashed through their air locks, their farms, and their hatcheries. How would people have acted if a giant monster stumbled into Berlin?

"Surgery is done in thirty seconds," Ben said. "Looks good. Your arm will be sore for a few days."

"If you're lucky, I'll share my meds with you."

"Ha."

She decided she could do better than joke. "No, I'm serious," she said. "Take out most of the nerve blocks. I need to use my arm. Don't immobilize it."

The AI shut off thirty percent of the numbing agents.

"More. Stop," she said when it hit fifty percent. She flexed her arm and grimaced.

Silently, the AI extracted its probes. They'd ordered it to communicate with her via data and imagery on her display, which Tom couldn't see. Originally she'd also used an implant to listen to her crewmates. They hadn't wanted to frighten Tom by broadcasting disembodied voices into the module, but he'd sensed the murmur of her implant, which confused him because their voices rarely matched her demeanor. Koebsch tended to worry. Ben offered wry humor and encouragement. Meanwhile, crewmates like Ash, Henri, and Harmeet ranged in attitudes of disgust toward the sunfish to bright fascination.

Vonnie had limited her radio channels to two men. She craved Ben's support, and Koebsch was the boss, so she couldn't stop him from barking at her when he disapproved.

As the medical AI posted green bars on her display, Koebsch said, "Von, if Tom hurts you again..."

"He might."

"You don't have to do this. We should be using mecha for our ambassadors."

She continued to massage Tom's topside. "Koebsch, we've tried mecha," she said. "This is better. It's more productive."

"You're too vulnerable in there."

"It's necessary. Face to face is how the sunfish approach everything."

"Nobody wants to see you get killed," Koebsch said, and Ben added, "Well, some people do."

Vonnie laughed.

For everyone who called her a hero for her role in the ESA's breakthroughs with the sunfish, others had condemned her as an idiot, a would-be martyr, or a traitor to the human race.

Fortunately, most of the crew stood in her corner. Sometimes they'd jeopardized their careers to help her, although they had the unusual advantage of being irreplaceable. Their leaders in Berlin could dock their pay or issue reprimands, but at the moment, Jupiter and Earth were nearly on opposite sides of the sun. Radio signals took thirty-eight minutes to travel in one direction. The crew had more independence than Berlin wanted, which put Koebsch in the difficult spot of enforcing his protocols on real-time situations.

"Von, this isn't funny," Koebsch said.

"If you die, Koebsch is in trouble," Ben explained, trying again to make her laugh at the other man's expense.

Vonnie frowned uneasily at their competition. "We can argue later," she said. "Please. Let me work. If you look at my display, I'm making progress. Tom and I are closer now. Our fight was actually good for us."

Koebsch grunted, but he said nothing else. She was correct. The translation AIs had doubled her affinity scores, which calculated her rapport with Tom based on a thousand factors from voice intonations to skin temperatures.

Hour by hour, Vonnie was learning to think more like a sunfish while Tom acted more human.

She eased his weight from her leg, then stood up, keeping her toes in contact with two of his arms. "Sing with me," she said. "Sing." Then she danced. "*Danach lasst uns alle streben, Brüderlich mit Herz and Hand...*"

Tom chirped and swayed, matching her cadence.

"*Einigkeit under Recht and Frieheit, Sind des Glückes Unterpfand.*"

Three years of clarinet lessons in a Frankfurt elementary school had been Vonnie's highest musical training. Her singing voice was raw at best. Ben said she sounded like a boy. Tom cared more about emotion than harmony. Resynchronizing the moods of every tribe member after a battle or a hunting party's return was a sunfish ritual.

They moved together.

The experience was surreal, singing with an alien inside a man-made structure on another world. It was magical. It surpassed her childhood dreams of visiting distant stars at lightspeed.

I may be the luckiest woman alive, she thought, glancing at the cues on her display. She tended to forget the lyrics of trendy songs, which was why she repeated Germany's national anthem, having memorized it long ago when her mother enrolled her in those clarinet lessons.

Koebsch had urged her to change her repertoire. Politics over-shadowed every move they made. Back on Earth, thousands of citizens and hundreds of officials had objected to what they viewed as Vonnie's nationalism, so she'd varied her play list with the anthems of France, Britain and the U.S., mangling her French but having fun with a mock British accent. Once she'd tried some limericks Ben had taught her.

People got upset about everything. People were self-centered and self-absorbed. The sunfish were selfless. For them, the tribe was paramount. They were maniacal in their devotion to the whole — they went too far — but Vonnie admired their purity.

She believed Tom had been partnered with her for the same reasons he'd served his tribe as a scout. He was remarkably independent for a male, durable and smart. With his severed arm, he was also a cripple and therefore expendable.

The matriarchs of his clan hadn't expected him to emerge in one piece from Submodule 07. The joke was Vonnie's superiors had also doubted she would survive.

The greatest similarity between humans and sunfish was that they ruled their respective food chains because they were paranoid, adaptable omnivores. Their greatest difference was that the sunfish did not — could not — lie. They had no modesty. In combat, they'd mastered ambushes and trickery, but their bodies were their language like living Braille. They did not have hidden motives or subconscious thoughts. Their minds were a fluid ballet. Everything they felt, they exhibited in a staccato rush.

VONNIE: Show me trust / My tribe is strong.

TOM: You show fear.

VONNIE: You hurt me / I can help.

TOM: Show fear / Taste good.

VONNIE: *<concealing new fear>* No / Trust / Don't hurt me / My tribe is strong.

TOM: More tools / More food.

VONNIE: Tools / Food / Yes / We can give you food and tools / Show trust.

TOM: You show fear.

"He can't get past it," Ben said on her display, adding a guarded tone to their dance.

"He can," Vonnie said. "He will."

TOM: Many voices / Other voices / Your tribe shows fear.

VONNIE: Show trust / My tribe can help / Help you / My lover possesses me.

TOM: My tribe possesses me.

VONNIE: *<indicating embarrassment>* Don't listen / Don't / I show trust.

"Oh shit, did you see that?" she asked.

Ben chuckled and said, "Yeah. It's funny what slips through."

"Don't laugh at me."

"I'm not," Ben said, but she heard the grin in his voice. It made her annoyed and glad, a conflict of feelings that intrigued the sunfish.

TOM: You spurn him / Want him / Are you fertile?

VONNIE: No / Show embarrassment.

TOM: *<indicating confusion>* You mate with him / Your smell / Your heat / Are you fertile?

VONNIE: He protects me / Pleasures me / Embarrassment.

"Gah," she said, struggling with her loss of composure. She wondered how many scientists and administrators would review her transcripts on Earth, but Tom didn't comprehend her urge for secrecy.

TOM: You show surprise / You don't know you?

VONNIE: I know / They see / Small shame / Large pride / My tribe sees shame and failure inside large pride.

TOM: Humans and sunfish / Treaty / Show pride.

VONNIE: Yes / Show pride.

She smiled at Tom's mental leap. He often found her puzzling or dense, but he'd learned to sift through her surface thoughts. He'd identified the heart of her feelings. Her embarrassment was less important than her conviction or her sense of accomplishment, and he shared her desire to work through their differences.

TOM: Determination and trust.

VONNIE: Yes / Show trust / I can hide my lover from you.

TOM: *<indicating new suspicion>* Why hide / Where / I hear chaos in you.

VONNIE: Impatience / Chagrin.

TOM: You are distant from yourself.

VONNIE: No / Show trust.

TOM: I hear distance and chaos in you.

VONNIE: Stop.

Folding her arms in a pose that meant *wait*, she took a breath. Tom was swift to perceive nuances she'd barely seen in herself. Trying to keep up with him was dizzying. Too often he led her into spirals of negative feedback, pressuring her, digging and gnawing at her like she was a tunnel in the ice.

"Don't worry about me," Ben said. "Tell him whatever you want."

"I shouldn't," she said.

"You have to."

She nodded pensively. "All right." So she tried to dance about human lust, explaining this side of herself.

Vonnie and Ben hadn't violated regulations by sleeping to-gether. The ESA knew it couldn't require adults to live in isolation for years without sexual relationships. In fact, their agency's leaders had balanced the crew's genders and ages with the certainty that some of them would pair up, and maybe break up, while others adopted the roles of mediators or rivals or confidants. Healthy people needed romance. The tensions it created were a driving force in any group.

The problem was Vonnie had become a celebrity. How she cut her hair or which books she read during breakfast were the subjects of endless debate. Fan clubs had voted for her to sleep with various men (and women) on Europa.

Her detractors were waiting for a mistake. Offending the sunfish with her sexual activities would serve as the ideal crime for certain politicians and faith-based leaders. Part of her also worried about getting Koebsch in trouble. Would their slight mutual attraction show through?

Mostly she didn't want to hurt Ben. What if he was humiliated by what she revealed to the world?

She didn't think she loved him. He felt more like a great friend, good in bed, great at his job, great on the radio and great in their labs. They worked together, so she wanted a little separation from him. The mission came first. But she thought he loved her. He was too protective.

It wasn't fair for his passion or her softer affection to become public news, so she tried to inject more into her voice and body than she'd genuinely experienced.

VONNIE: Excitement / Satisfaction.
TOM: I hear more voices in you.

VONNIE: Yes / Guilt / Respect.

TOM: You are chaotic and weak.

VONNIE: We are not sunfish.

TOM: <*indicating fear of a quake*> You are unstable.

VONNIE: No / Yes.

TOM: Wait.

Vonnie shouldn't have laughed. For once, it seemed like she'd overwhelmed Tom rather than the other way around. He retreated from her with his arms curled against his sides. Then her laughter stopped. With dismay, she realized he was signaling an end to their session.

She followed him across the module with her arms down, mimicking his shape, shuffling her feet when she could have run to cut him off. "Come back," she said.

VONNIE: Listen and talk.

TOM: No / Go.

VONNIE: Listen!

TOM: Go.

She knew better than to crowd him, not unless she wanted more wounds. He pounded at a latch installed specifically for him on the floor. It opened a small, customized air lock leading out of Submodule 07.

"Tom!" she said. Then she turned and called, "What did I miss?"

"His last readings seemed positive," Ben said.

"What if it's a negotiating tactic?" Koebsch asked.

The AIs translated Tom's mood as matter-of-fact. The sunfish were never apologetic, but Vonnie thought she sensed sadness. Maybe she was projecting.

Tom entered the lock and closed the door, leaving her by

herself in 07.

"Do we have more food for him?" she asked.

"Roger that," Ben said. "We set another container outside while you were talking. We've prepped others, but he can only carry one by himself."

"He could tell his tribe," she said. "They'd come back for more."

"Do you want me to slow the lock or send a mecha around to meet him?"

"No. Don't slow the lock. He knows how long the cycle takes."

"The outer door is opening now."

"Don't send our mecha, either," Koebsch said. "He might think they're a threat."

"Damn it." Feeling lost, Vonnie paced away from Tom's air lock and said, "Cameras. Full grid. I want to see what he's doing."

"Get back to the surface," Koebsch said.

"I will." She traced her good hand through her display, holographically enhancing the best angles without moving her exterior sensors. If a single lens swiveled or zoomed, Tom would notice. She didn't want him to feel like he was being hunted.

She wondered if something had happened outside. Were other sunfish calling him?

Watching her display, Vonnie saw nothing unusual. Suspended by its struts and mooring cables, Submodule 07 perched at one end of a man-made cavern in the ice. Above it and alongside it, two steel shafts connected the cavern with the surface. The first was an access tube for people. It opened into Hab Module 06, a new structure they'd built above 07. The second was a larger cargo tube. It led to a staging area for mecha.

At the other end of the cavern, the ice crumbled. Narrow

cracks led into an eroding maze where the few open spaces fell toward a larger series of catacombs forty meters below.

Tom had stopped breathing as soon as he left 07 for the toxic air outside. Sunfish hemoglobin was a twisted iron-rich protein, which allowed them to retain spectacular concentrations of oxygen. Tom could run two kilometers without another breath. Because he had gills in addition to lungs, he could also endure on puddles if necessary or fully submerged in rivers or seas.

In infrared, he was a graceful star surrounded by the frigid bulk of the ice. Vonnie watched him leap through a short, perfect arc. He sailed to the thirty-kilo metal container they'd left for him.

He grabbed it. He screeched. Then he flung himself across the cavern with his prize. The AIs interpreted his cry as challenging and triumphant, even warlike.

Why?

Fifteen times before, Tom had reported back to his matriarchs. It was conceivable that this meeting — their sixteenth — marked a vital step. The sunfish counted in twos and eights like human beings counted in fives and tens. Vonnie's crewmates believed his tribe was approaching a decision of some kind, but she couldn't fathom why Tom had waited until now to press her about Ben.

Days ago, he'd learned every detail of her anatomy in his shameless, unpretentious way. During their first meetings, Koebsch had also allowed Tom to interact with a few types of mecha, which thrilled him more than any human.

The sunfish revered power. They had been stunned to discover people controlled mecha, not vice versa. Understanding the symbiosis of man and machine had led Vonnie and Tom through several discussions about life on Earth. The idea of nations was similar to that of tribes. More alien to him were the concepts of monogamous sex and children born to one couple, especially because human civilization was rife with adultery, divorce, abuse and neglect.

Reporting to his matriarchs, Tom must have shared every trait he'd discerned in Vonnie and the voices of her friends. She hoped his impressions were favorable. The sunfish had enjoyed the ESA's lavish gifts of tools and food, but they always thought in the short term.

What if they'd decided a few gifts were enough?

Bypassing the nearest gaps in the cavern floor, Tom brought his container to a wider chasm. He disappeared into the maze. Soon he would travel out of range.

Vonnie's crewmates had seeded the ice with spies, yet they remained blind in thirty percent of the immediate area. Two disasters had cost them hundreds of mecha. They were still building new rovers and probes to meet their needs.

Because they couldn't afford to lose any resources, they had been cautious to infiltrate while Tom and other scouts were gone. Then the sagging ice in the maze had pinned several of their machines, crushing one of their hard-won mecha and immobilizing four more.

The larger catacombs below Submodule 07 were uncharted territory. Somehow his tribe had identified and destroyed every beacon hidden in the ESA's containers. Previously, other sunfish had chewed nanotags from their own skin. Now the ESA's containers were free of devices. The AIs had said her crew was losing Tom's trust by attempting — and failing — to deceive him.

So much of what we do is false or two-faced, Vonnie thought.

She worried that she might not see him again. *We may be too complicated for them to accept. We're so loud in our heads, so convoluted in our social groups.*

"I'm sorry," she said. Her words were for Tom even though he was gone.

Both men answered. "You were fantastic," Ben said.

"Get to the surface," Koebsch told her. "I don't like how Tom screamed before he left."

"The AIs think it sounded like goodbye," she said.

"It was more than that," Koebsch said. "There were some aspects of goodbye in his arm movements, but his scream was defiant. It was aggressive. Get to the surface or I'll pull the whole module."

"That would ruin everything."

"Do you remember what happened to Pärnits and Collins-worth? The sunfish don't need to kill you themselves. If they open another geyser..."

"Our sensors would hear them digging."

"Not if they're too far down."

"Koebsch, they know when I leave the module. If Tom challen-ged me and I retreat, it demonstrates weakness. Let me stay. We need to show confidence."

"The sunfish could have caused the tremor. They could be preparing another collapse."

"Ben, what do your models say?" Vonnie asked.

"His models weren't predicting a quake and he can't explain where it originated," Koebsch said. "Get out. You can go back after we see what happens."

"What's happening is I let him down," Vonnie said. "We need

to try harder, not expect them to figure everything out for us."

"Look. Don't be so hard on yourself." Koebsch's voice was encouraging now. "Nobody else is willing to walk in there with a sunfish," he said. "You've been exceptional, but I'll be damned if I'm going to watch more of my people die. Get out or I'll pull the module."

Vonnie nodded reluctantly as she walked to the escape hatch. "Yes, sir," she said. Then she opened the locker that held her boots and gloves, delaying as long as possible, wanting to stay and needing to go.

Nothing on Europa was easy.

3.

Jupiter, a gas giant, was almost large enough to have ignited as a dwarf star. It formed a miniature solar system unto itself. It had seventy-one moons in addition to three rings of collisional debris and ejecta. Many of its satellites were mere rubble — stray, dead rocks it had swept up from space — but its four major moons resembled the planets orbiting the sun.

They were as big as Mercury. They had Earth-like molten cores, water, and strange atmospheres.

Unfortunately, they belonged to Jupiter's busy inner system. Io, Europa, Ganymede, and Callisto circled their father like tormented sisters.

For the most part, Jupiter's rings consisted of particles finer than smoke, but its rings were unsteady and released vast tendrils of dust. The moons had been sand-blasted for eons. More violently, millions of asteroids swung in and out of the moons' paths. All of them were scarred by craters with a single exception. Europa. Her salt water ocean, which swallowed her completely, kept her exterior from preserving the damage caused by meteor impacts.

At temperatures of -162° Celsius, Europa's surface ice was twenty kilometers thick in places. It drifted on the equator and twisted at the poles, buckling, folding. Meanwhile, orbital stresses caused volcanic activity inside her molten core. Magma and gas created soft spots and melts. The smallest meteor impacts vanished rapidly. The largest opened floods.

Europa was covered with ridges and cracks and blemishes. Nevertheless, she was smooth compared to the other moons. Like Earth, she had weather and erosion, although her feeble weather systems varied among the catacombs within the ice. Her true storms existed in her ocean, which no Earth-made probes had ever seen.

Neither men nor mecha had traveled deeper than four kilometers. The ice was too treacherous, and they were still evaluating the sunfish.

They'd designed Submodule 07 because their efforts to coax an ambassador above the surface had failed. First they'd relocated the camp they shared with the FNEE — Brazil's *Força Nacional de Exploração do Espaço* — moving to within five kilometers of the sunfish colony. They'd left a handful of sensors in the chasms beneath their old camp, after which they'd required a single day to move everything else because they owned so few pieces of equipment.

Developing the new site had taken longer. Using mecha, the ESA had explored several catacombs. Then they'd needed twelve days to seal the ice with pressure tents, excavate, insert 07 with its access and cargo tubes, and repack the surface. When they were done, they'd spent nine more days and a hundred kilos of food luring scouts like Tom back into the area.

As expected, the noise of their diggers had chased off every bug and sunfish for three cubic kilometers. The biologists had established that even the native fungi released spores as if trying to run when subjected to quakes or severe drops in atmospheric pressure. That was why the ESA hadn't dug near Tom's home, a location they'd mapped in detail. His tribe might have fled or declared war. Europan lifeforms feared blowouts on the surface more than geysers or magma from below. Floods and fire could be survived. The vacuum of space was literally the end of their world.

The sunfish had never imagined anything beyond the ice. Their total lack of curiosity at First Contact had caused many factions on Earth to doubt their intelligence. They simply regarded people as another lifeform. For tens of thousands of years, the tribes had met bizarre creatures from separate ecologies in the ice. Every-thing was food. Even their unfamiliarity with metal and electronics hadn't stopped them from attacking.

Later, they'd accepted the mecha as superior beings. In fact, it wasn't until the mecha demonstrated obedience to Vonnie that Tom had addressed her with the same esteem he gave his matriarchs.

The sunfish understood master-slave relationships. They took prisoners during their wars with each other — but while many prisoners were killed and eaten, others were absorbed into the conquering tribe as mates. Some became matriarchs in time.

Among the sunfish, adaptability came second only to their hair-trigger willingness to fight.

Tom's tribe, Top Clan Eight-Six, had accepted a treaty with the ESA. The sunfish were desperate for resources. The ESA wanted allies to teach them about Europa's history; envoys to introduce them to more tribes; and guides to lead them further into the catacombs.

Vonnie believed they'd made substantial progress. Was it enough? Their leaders on Earth were anxious. The mission costs had been steep — and they'd barely gotten started. Establishing peace and exploring Europa were enormous tasks with no end in sight.

The situation was further complicated by the reality that humankind was no more unified than the sunfish. ESA, American, Brazilian and Chinese mecha had explored different regions beneath the surface, and neither altruism nor pure science had been their goals. Earth's crews had launched electronic attacks against each other as they maneuvered for position and for political gain. Brazilian mecha had engaged three sunfish tribes in combat, intending to secure live specimens until the sunfish tore open a volcanic hot springs like a doomsday bomb.

The result had been hundreds killed among the tribes and two more human deaths. Vonnie knew it could happen again. The promises made between the ESA and Top Clan Eight-Six were as fragile as the ice itself.

4.

The red emergency lights in 07 switched on as Vonnie touched an abort sequence on her display. Above her, the escape hatch opened with a *clang*. The sound felt like defeat. The sunfish were always listening. Their scouts would tell the matriarchs she'd left the module, so she tried again. "Koebsch, I should stay."

"No," he said. "Tom retreated. Why can't you?"

"We've positioned ourselves as the dominant group. We want to dictate terms to them, not run when we're nervous."

"You aren't thinking. If they take offense because you left, we can handle another setback. But if we lose you, that will end our treaty."

Vonnie paused, marveling at his ability to outwit her with his prudent by-the-book logic. What he'd said was accurate. If the tribes killed anyone else, Earth might permanently dismiss the idea of collaborating with them.

"All right, I'm climbing up," she said.

"Good. Tom will come back if they're not planning an attack. They need us."

Do they? she wondered.

She scaled the ladder on the module wall. It led into the access

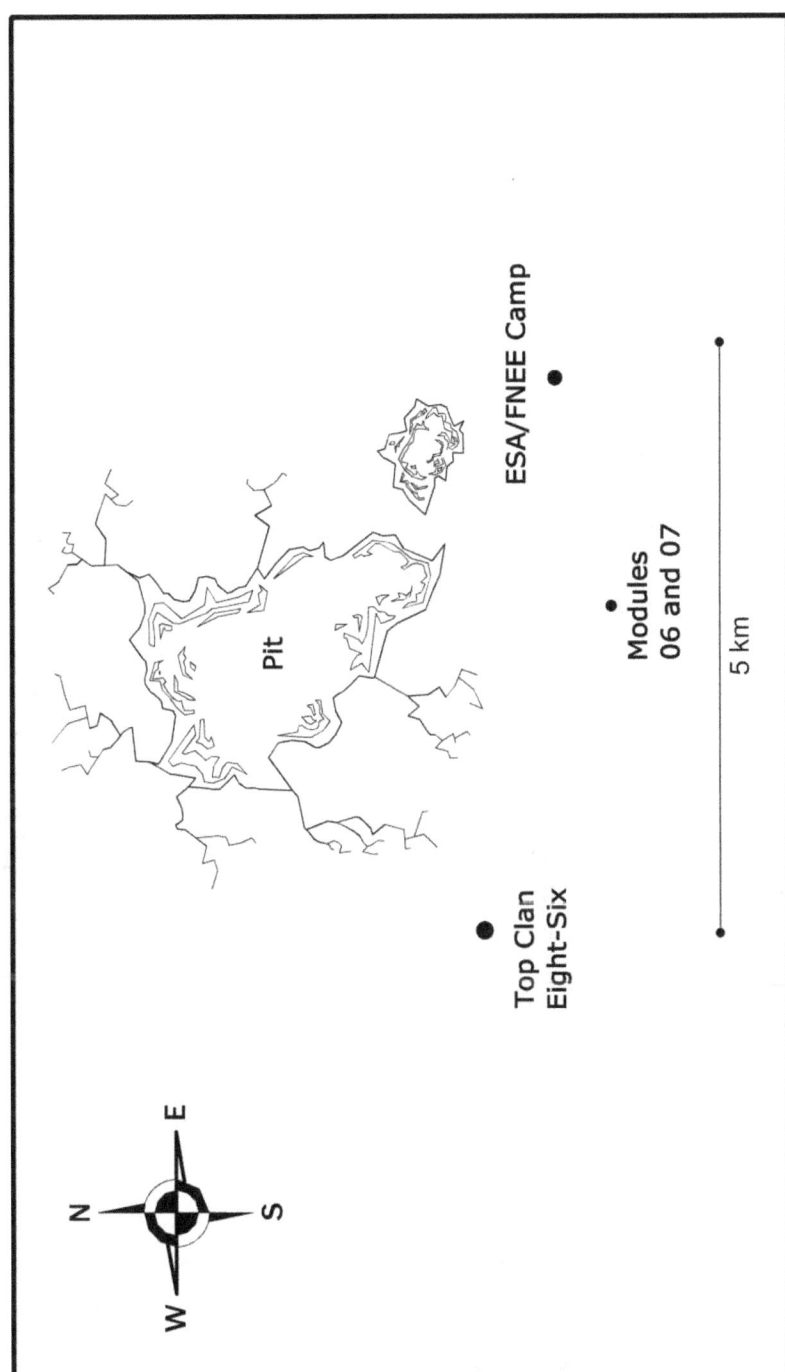

Surface of the Southern Pole

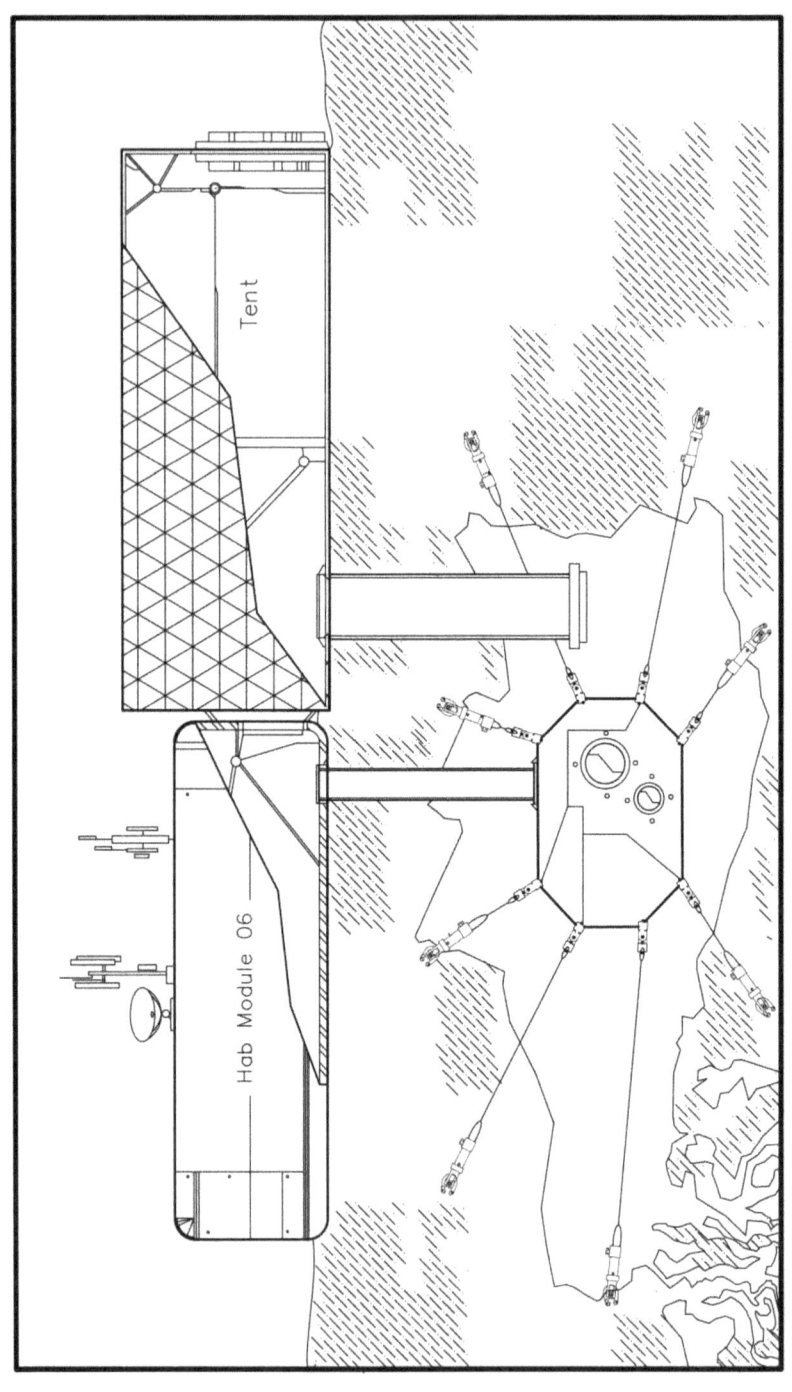

Submodule 07

tube, and she moved delicately, aware of every whisper and bang of her hands and feet.

Ben had tested the tribe's vigilance by using mecha to create infrasound and tapping patterns on the surface. Then he'd rewarded Tom and other scouts with food for reproducing his signals. Their hearing was exceptional, which explained their uncanny grasp of spatial relations.

On Earth, the ground reflected sound waves like an invisible topography map, enabling birds to exist in an acoustic landscape unknown to people.

On Europa, the noise was all-encompassing. The sunfish had adapted. Their many ears, encircling their bodies, allowed them to measure specific wave-lengths as well as the location of each source. More astounding was their reaction time. From neurological scans and autopsies, Ben thought sunfish could anticipate the path of human footsteps from one step to the next. If the ice was calm, they could do so from a distance of a full kilometer while differentiating among several targets at once. As a biologist, Ben had his own particular affection for the sunfish, but he also called them *spooky little mothers*.

He spoke on her data/comm relay as she sealed 07 beneath her, closing the hatch on its roof. "Hurry up," he said.

"I'm coming."

"Do it faster," he said. "We're hearing some new activity. You don't want to be in the tube if the feces strike the oscillating rotor."

"What?"

"The shit might hit the fan. Get out."

Vonnie felt her eyes widen. She scrambled up, clanging on the steel rungs. She no longer cared about being quiet. Meds and counseling had helped her with her memories of her run beneath the ice, but she remained prone to claustrophobia.

The dim tube felt like a dead-end, a trap. She couldn't move fast enough.

Ben opened the top hatch with a *boom*, bathing her in the stark light of Hab Module 06. Wincing at the light, she missed the next rung. Her bad arm tangled with the ladder rungs.

"Von!" he called.

She caught herself and climbed. Her hands cast wild shadows on her face.

They'd darkened 07 in another effort to comfort Tom. Despite not having eyes, sunfish preferred blackness. Ben thought there were crude photoreceptors among their pedicellaria. The sunfish had dealt with magma flows since the beginning of time. He'd also suggested the ice might contain as-yet-undiscovered lifeforms who used bioluminescence. If the sunfish were preyed upon by such animals, natural selection would have favored the ability to evade their glow.

The sunfish hated light. Vonnie adored it. As she scrambled into 06, the light felt like home.

The access tube from 07 led into an armored chamber with one exit — a heavy air lock like a blast door. Ben closed the hatch behind her. They embraced and she closed her eyes, enjoying the pleasant salt smell of him.

She probably stank of adrenaline and blood. Ben didn't seem to mind. He kissed her and said, "Let's go."

She followed him out of the armored chamber. She started toward data/comm until he stopped to secure the air lock. He touched its *seal* and *alarm* commands as if he expected sunfish to swarm up through the tube.

"Christ," she said. "Are they inside 07?"

"It's just a precaution. We probably have some time, but we're securing all doors."

"Tell me where they are."

"They're going down, not up. They're digging. I can show you." He took her hand.

They walked into data/comm, a narrow room lined with two stations on each side. Three of the stations were empty. Standing in the fourth display was an old man. Tall and thin, he moved like a heron, pecking at his data packets with his index finger. He looked harmless.

At her first sight of him, Vonnie tugged free from Ben and raised her fists exactly as she'd done with Tom. "Dawson," she snarled. "What are you doing here?"

The old man didn't bother to meet her eyes. "Shush," he said. "Don't be juvenile."

"You drove across camp while I was in 07 with Tom right after a quake? Your jeep coming toward us might have been what frightened him!"

"Our rovers are always on the move."

"I told you to stay in 02."

"We have every right to travel among the modules as we choose. You're not—"

Ben intervened. He led her past Dawson and said, "Take this station. Von? Take this station. I'll patch you into my feed."

Vonnie bit back another remark and obeyed. She took off the light gloves she'd donned to climb out of 07. Then she held out her palm. Her handprint activated the station and filled it with her mem files and preferences, which followed her through every module, vehicle and suit in camp.

She couldn't stop herself from glancing again at Dawson. He could also access any device in camp. He had no reason to enter 06 except to physically intimidate her, did he?

The men couldn't have been more different. Ben Metzler was a short, blocky Austrian with a face like a bulldog and the rude mouth to match. Gossip personalities on the net had chided Vonnie for perpetuating the cliché of the beauty and the beast since she was lean and blond, but Ben wasn't a softy and he didn't have a heart of gold. He hated Dawson, too.

William George Dawson acted like a British lord. He was debonair. He'd also coldly ignored the signs of intelligence among the sunfish. He was a genesmith, and, to him, their DNA represented fortune and fame. Beneath his urbane facade, he was just another greedy asshole.

He's a snake.

Vonnie flexed in her display, opening a dozen new sims from Ben. According to their spies and surface mecha, the sunfish had fled *en masse* with Tom. The tribe's sounds were fading into the ice. It felt like part of her was leaving, too.

We can't reach them now, not unless we amplify our signals. We could shout into the ice... but if something scared them, screaming won't do any good.

She switched to camp telemetry and scrolled backward, identifying the movements of Dawson's jeep. He had driven slowly and in a straight line. He'd entered 06 almost three minutes before Tom left her. *That's a long time to a sunfish*, she thought, hanging her head in doubt.

"Do you think it was something I did?" she asked Ben under her breath.

"Von, they're so weird," he began. He was prepared to make excuses for her. He wanted to commiserate with her, but Dawson had heard.

"Still punishing yourself, I see," Dawson said.

Vonnie snarled and examined Ben's real-time sims, ignoring Dawson, furious that she'd lowered her guard. The old man used words like dabs of cyanide. He poisoned his foes with his little mind games.

His comment reminded her of what Koebsch had said. *Don't be so hard on yourself.*

Was there truth in it? Yes and no.

Among those who called her a traitor were others who'd labeled her a masochist. They said she defended the sunfish to benefit her broken ego. Some people claimed she'd helped the sunfish over her own race, which was a lie. The interests of a few money-grubbing men weren't the interests of humankind. She couldn't stop them from belittling her to make themselves look better, but she resented their slander. It was more than petty. It was criminal. Why couldn't they accept the exotic mysteries of this world?

She needed Top Clan Eight-Six to return. If not, her opponents would cite their disappearance as proof that engaging the sunfish was a worthless expense. And if they attacked...

"Look at this," she told Ben. "Our mecha beneath the FNEE module are picking up increased noise and radar activity. The tribe is circling north."

"They're moving toward us!" Dawson said.

"The primary catacombs bend in our direction," she said. "That's why we chose this site. The tribe must be coming closer as a temporary detour or a feint. They won't go near our surface emplacements."

"They will if they've readied an assault," Dawson said. "You can be sure they know how to bring us down like a house of cards. If they're good at anything, it's finding every weak point in the ice."

"Shut up, Dawson."

He shook his head theatrically. He knew she had a short fuse with father figures like Koebsch and so many of the politicians on Earth. His lectures were another calculated ploy to rile her.

Don't play his game, she thought, searching her display for evidence to prove him wrong. She still had one card up her sleeve. She wanted to shove it in his face.

Or shove him outside without a suit.

Like he'd said, the ESA crew were allowed anywhere in camp except two restricted labs. Even those could be entered with masks. They needed their freedom to keep from going stir-crazy. The floors of their hab modules were twenty meters by five, the landers fifteen by fifteen, and they'd had only five of these tiny homes to start, then four.

Module 03 had been crushed during the blowout caused by the sunfish. In honor of Collinsworth and Pärnits, the number 03 had been retired. The newly built structures were labeled 06 and 07, and no one except Vonnie and Tom went into 07. That meant the three modules — 01, 02 and 06 — and the landers — 04 and 05 — were their total living space.

Predictably, the nine people caught in the same few rooms

had separated themselves into special friendships and cliques. Each had staked out a particular spot as their own. They often mingled in the common area of the dining room in 02, yet tried to respect the unspoken boundaries around Ben and Vonnie's bed in 04 or the armory in 01 where Ash, Henri and O'Neal tinkered with their suits and other gadgets.

Dawson's lair was B Lab in 02. He was a loner. His closest acquaintance had been Collinsworth. Now only Koebsch would put up with him. Dawson had colleagues and fans on Earth, but the ESA psychologists hoped to rekindle a broader sense of team cohesion. They'd ordered Vonnie to attend AI-directed chats with Dawson to solve their conflicts.

Not a chance.

She'd hacked the AI before their first session. Instead of welcoming him at the appointed time, the AI had played her favorite clip from their worst fight — a clip of herself calling Dawson a liar and a mercenary.

On the media channels, their feud was almost as popular as the recordings of the blowout. She and Dawson should have been insignificant. They were standing on a moon inhabited by aliens! But to many people, the science was boring. They wanted human heroes and villains. Plenty of commentators entertained their audiences by choosing sides, which was why Vonnie dashed on some make-up and changed into a clean uniform before every interview.

Human beings had evolved to judge an impressive array of visual cues. That meant they could be shallow when they ignored their other senses. Some people supported her because she was pretty. Others disliked her for the same reason. She couldn't win.

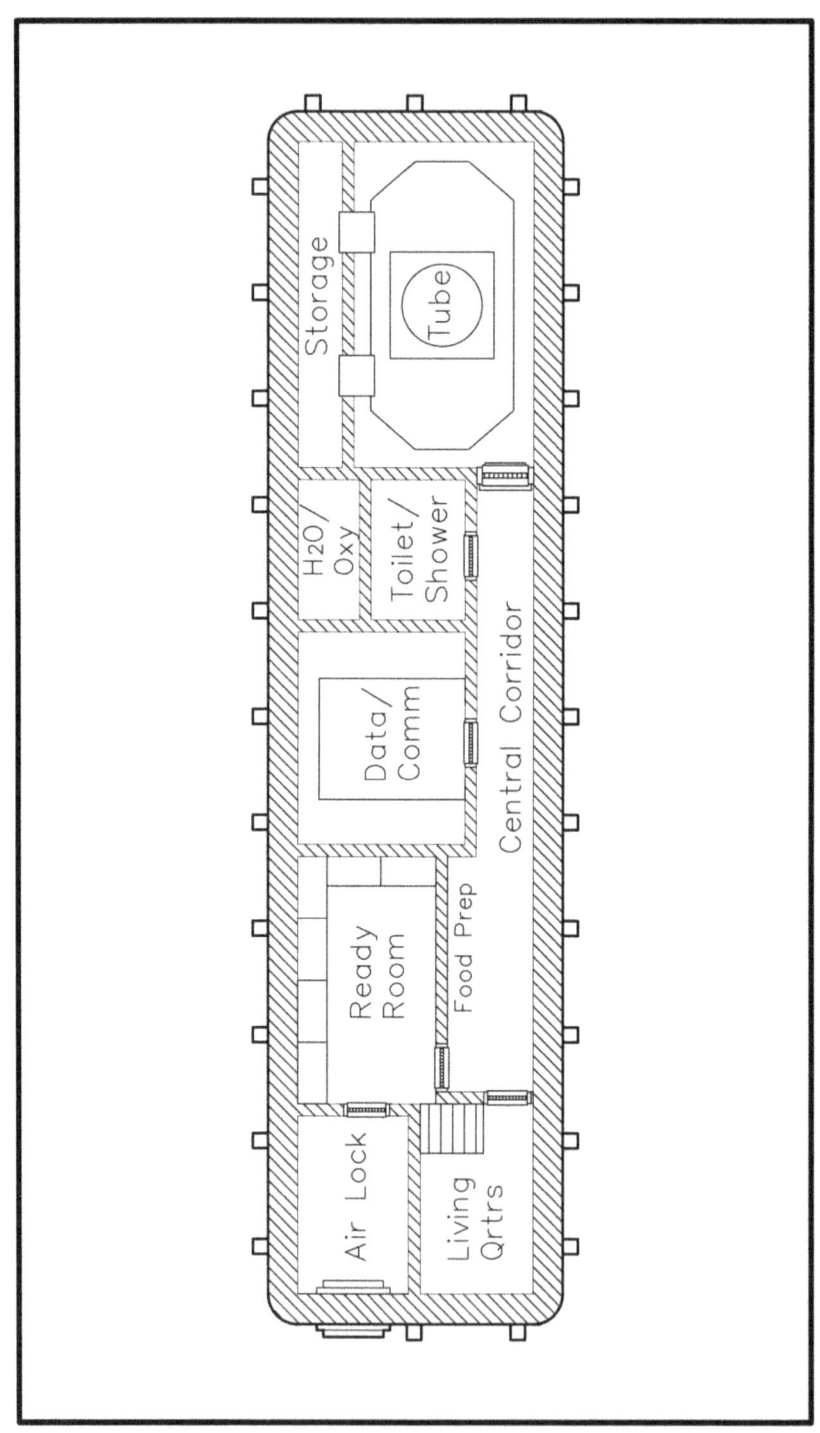

Hab Module 06

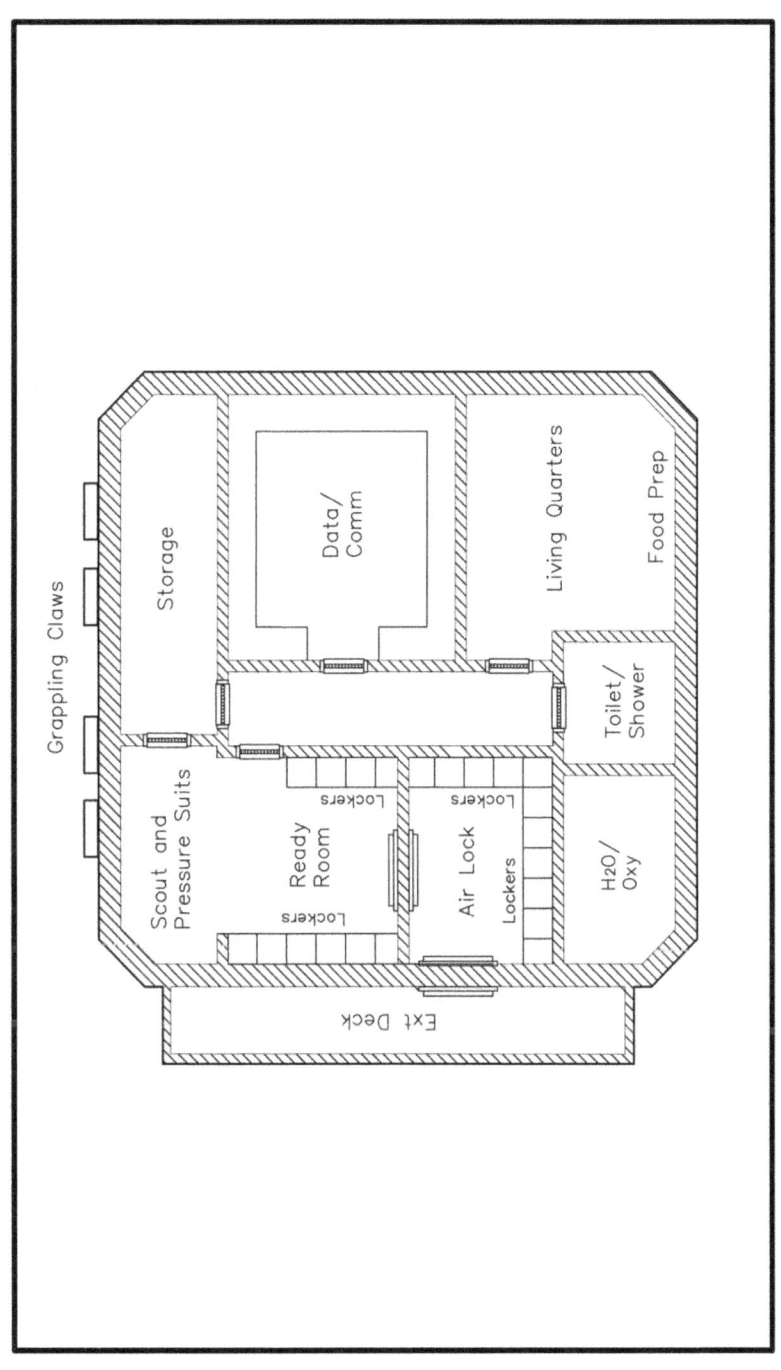

Lander 04

She'd tried to present herself as a no-nonsense, hardworking engineer (which was how she saw herself) until the ESA publicists screamed that her approval ratings had faltered; she was damaging the mission's visibility on the net; why had she scrubbed her face and who'd told her to wear coveralls instead of dress blues?

Her race was so insincere. More and more, she valued the sunfish for their frankness. Even when she couldn't grasp their motives, she knew they were acting in concert with each other.

"The tribe is already two kilometers down?" she asked.

"It might be three," Ben said. "We think their scouts are farther ahead of the main group than normal."

"They can't dig that fast."

"They had an escape route. It was covered with enough ice to blur it from our sensors. Then they opened it and ran. They were prepared for this."

"But we had a treaty," she said. "We've been feeding them. We were talking."

"The sunfish will always quit," Dawson said. "They can't accept our superiority. Too many of them are stupid animals, and the matriarchs don't want the others to overturn their social order with our technology."

"Fuck off, Billy."

She made sure she was broadcasting on her public channels to Earth before she spoke. If he wanted to play games, she could play games.

Billy was his least favorite diminutive of *William*. She also didn't want him to track her next moves.

As a diversion, cursing at him worked. Dawson called Koebsch.

"Administrator, really," he said. "Miss Vonderach is again subjecting me to her primitive verbal abuse."

"Stop it, Von," Koebsch said.

"Yes, sir." She smiled. Her primitive verbal abuse was a crowd pleaser with everyone who'd felt the sting of Dawson's arrogance. Some of his allies would probably laugh behind his back, too. They weren't his friends. They were corporate shills who needed his expertise or whack jobs of various political stripes.

Then her smile faded. *I should feel bad for him*, she thought. *He's seventy-three and he's spent his life wrapped up in his own intellect. Never married. No children. How smart is that? Too smart. I don't want to end up like him, all job, no family. Why can't I let Ben closer to me?*

Looking at her boyfriend, Vonnie realized how thoroughly she'd grown to expect his support. Believing in him was a fine emotion. She raised a privacy screen to conceal herself from Dawson and touched five coordinates on her map. "You know what I'm thinking, right?"

"I do." Ben nodded, but his tone was flirtatious. Marriage jokes were his favorite method of teasing her.

"We can't let Dawson find out," she said.

"Relax. I made sure he didn't fox our data/comm when he came inside. Our channels are secure, and Tavares is online if you need her."

"I do." Vonnie grinned mischievously when his mouth fell open in surprise.

She turned back to her display. Most of the FNEE and ESA crews were present on the group feed. Vonnie wanted to speak with Tavares and O'Neal, but Sergeant Claudia Tavares was the low woman on the Brazilians' totem pole. Vonnie required Colonel Ribeiro's permission to talk to her, so she tapped O'Neal's feed instead. He was in Command Module 01 with Koebsch and Ash.

"Where do you think the tribe is going?" she asked.

O'Neal shrugged. "Unknown. Too many possibilities. Koebsch is right that Tom's body language and his biochemistry seemed to indicate 'Goodbye.'"

"Was he reacting to Dawson's jeep?"

"Unknown." In his early fifties, O'Neal was a strapping Irishman with curly rust-brown hair. That was where the caricature ended. Unlike every stereotype of his countrymen, O'Neal had the temperament of a slug. His work thrilled him and he could chat about it for hours, but he was unflappable. His voice rarely lifted above a steady patter.

Like most of them, he'd earned a pile of degrees. Everyone except Dawson handled multiple jobs since it cost too much to send three people into space if one genius would do. O'Neal was a biologist/ecologist and assisted in engineering. After a series of crash courses, he'd also become their chief linguist to fill the void left by Pärnits and Collinsworth. That was why Vonnie had called him.

Reading from a window on her display, she said, "I don't understand your translation."

"Me either," O'Neal agreed. "Tom used new signs to indicate distance and time apart. Larger distances. Longer times. It doesn't look good, Von, not with the obvious challenge before he left."

"I can't believe they'd abandon us."

"The tribe was ready for him to join them and go. They pulled in their sentries. They sent new scouts ahead. Then they evacuated their eggs and tools. The choreography is breathtaking if you want to study it."

Vonnie envied his self-possession. O'Neal said *breathtaking* like he'd asked her to pass the wine at dinner.

"Can you tell me what they left behind?" she asked. "Is their home empty or did they leave caches of food? Did they set traps?"

"Radar shows all four entrances were rigged with deadfalls, then blocked."

"That means they're coming back."

"We can't be certain. Their home is a warm place they could reclaim years from now. The matriarchs might have left it for other tribes to find like a vault. It's too warm to preserve food or biologics, but trace elements could last for decades. The deadfalls are a test. Sunfish who aren't smart enough to avoid getting crushed won't get in."

Koebsch joined their conversation. "Look, this is interesting," he said. "I hope you're right, but nobody knows what the tribe is doing."

"They wouldn't bother to seal their home if they expected this area to be destroyed," Vonnie said.

"Cave-ins are unpredictable. A flood might undermine our camp but miss their home. They only needed a few minutes to seal it up. Maybe they're hedging their bets."

"Koebsch, I'm surprised at you. It made sense to pull me from 07, but you're talking like—"

"Von, I'm sorry. We're out of time." Avoiding her eyes, Koebsch activated a Class 1 alert on every data/comm line in camp. "Listen up," he said. "I've radioed Earth, but the soonest we'll hear back is fifty-six minutes. Meanwhile we have contingencies in place. I'm under orders to obey the top proxies. They've instructed me to activate our defenses."

Dawson nodded sagely on the group feed. "Wiser heads prevail," he said as Vonnie shouted, "You can't let AIs make that decision!"

"Those are my orders," Koebsch said.

"We're a civilian operation," Vonnie argued, which wasn't strictly correct. At least two of her crewmates served MI6 or the Directorate — British intelligence and French national security — and the FNEE team was military.

Recent agreements on Earth had united the astronauts of the European Union and Brazil. Each crew continued to live in their own modules and they maintained separate org charts, although Vonnie and Sergeant Tavares had been retasked as liaisons. They'd linked many of their databases and mecha, communicating with each other by showphone. Less often, a few individuals met in person in their labs or outside on the ice. The two groups had traded rations to bring variety to their meals. The FNEE soldiers were equally hungry for access to ESA entertainment channels to watch in their downtime.

Vonnie considered Tavares a friend. The sergeant's heart was in the right place. Unfortunately, Tavares was even more beholden to her superiors than Vonnie was to Koebsch. As a junior support tech, Tavares had zero clout, and Colonel Ribeiro must have been assigned to lead the FNEE team because he was devoted and competitive and stern.

There were only seven Brazilians on the ice (and one more who'd stayed in their spacecraft, trailing Europa as it orbited

Jupiter) compared to sixteen Americans, twenty-four Chinese, and the nine surviving members of the ESA crew.

Brazil was the weakest nation in space. They owned the smallest fleet and the grandest ambitions.

Ribeiro had personally controlled a gun platform during the FNEE assault on the tribes. Vonnie despised him. The ease with which he'd slain the sunfish was far worse than Dawson's greed.

"Don't do this," she said, but Koebsch said, "Colonel, you're in command of our mecha. My people are sending you access codes now."

"Acknowledged," Ribeiro said. His dark, taut face was expressionless except for the gleam in his eyes.

"Stop!" Vonnie cried.

"I want to lodge a formal protest," Ben said as she added, "Koebsch, putting us on high alert is the wrong thing to do. You're exacerbating the situation. The tribes will hear Ribeiro deploying our mecha."

Koebsch glanced at her with regret. Then he muted her feed, silencing her. "I need everyone in pressure suits," he said. "Prep our landers for takeoff. If the sunfish are moving toward another hot spring — if they open a geyser — we might have five minutes to evacuate."

5.

Vonnie, Ben and Dawson left their displays. They hurried out of data/comm into the corridor. Vonnie avoided Dawson's gaze, but the old man pursed his lips and said, almost kindly, "You're a fool, Von."

"Don't start with me."

"This is for your own good," he said.

Ten paces brought them to the ready room, the largest compartment in 06, which was jammed with equipment. Five lockers lined the wall. Vonnie didn't know what to make of Dawson's tone, so she was rude again.

"Just put on your suit," she said.

Dawson gestured for her and Ben to dress first. Each locker was designed to transfer the components of a pressure suit to its wearer with robot assists. In an emergency, they could throw on their suits anywhere, but the process went more smoothly with the assists. That meant two people at a time, and even two people were crowded.

Vonnie stripped off her tank top and shorts. She kept her bra but not her underwear as Ben removed his standard blue one-piece. He knocked her with his elbow. She bumped his hip when she stepped into the legs of her suit, then connected its sanitary features.

Dawson didn't wait because he wanted to see if I had pink or black undies today, she thought. Astronauts lived without privacy in their hab modules. He'd seen her undergoing her weekly physical. Hell, pirated copies of her Arianespace employee files had appeared on the net as soon as she was famous, and those files had included full body scans to monitor her health. Nude sims of Alexis Vonderach weren't hard to find.

Dawson's gallantry meant women and children first.

"Ha," she snickered, wondering what Ben would say if he realized Dawson viewed him as a boy. *Should I tell him? I could use a good fight. We can stuff my shirt in Dawson's pompous mouth...*

Her suit smelled like plastic, sweat and freshener. In Earth gravity, including her pack, it would have weighed 100 kilos. If necessary, it could keep her alive for days without recharging her air or water.

She donned her gloves, then took her helmet. She didn't put it on. They might wait inside their suits for hours, so she wanted to kiss Ben. She was glad they could be troublemakers together, but she wasn't comfortable showing physical affection in front of Dawson.

She flashed Ben a private look. "Let's get back to data/comm. We'll seal our helmets there."

"Seal them now," Dawson said.

"You should suit up," Ben told him. Ben was a sharp cookie. He knew what was in store for him as soon as they were alone, and his gaze shifted from Vonnie's face to her chest.

Dawson stopped her from leaving her locker. "How can you feel as if any of us are safe when you endured severe injuries not twenty minutes ago?" he asked. "That sunfish might have killed you."

Her mood darkened. "His name is Tom, and he didn't mean it like you or I would mean it," she said.

"That's my point. They're nothing like us."

"Get out of my way," she said.

"Seal your helmets," Dawson insisted.

Unexpectedly, her anger became something else. She'd experienced a trace of pity for him before. Now she felt grudging respect. "Thank you for letting us go first," she said before she walked away.

Just when I thought I had Dawson figured out, he really acts like a gentleman. He's always poured juice or wine for the women in the mess hall. I thought he was being chauvinistic. He's so oily. But he was trying to be courteous.

I remember when Harmeet had one of her migraines and Dawson went through his personal effects for that overpriced brandy he bought in Paris and wouldn't share with anyone. He said it might relax her, and Harmeet said she thought it did. Maybe he's only 98% asshole.

Brooding, Vonnie reentered data/comm. Ben appeared behind her. She glanced at her display, but she didn't approach it. She went to him.

They necked like teenagers — urgently, erotically — chuckling into each other's mouths at the shared frustration of petting their gloves on the firm mesh of the suits. It was like making love covered in plastic from shoulders to toes while holding her helmet under one arm, all foreplay, no satisfaction. He stroked her waist with his free hand. Heating up, she cupped his groin. He bit her neck and she whispered in his ear.

His favorite was oral sex. "I'll sixty-nine with you until our jaws hurt and you can't walk straight," she said. "I'll do anything you want."

"Stop." Ben laughed. "You better stop before my relief tube slips off." He meant he was growing erect.

She snickered again, licking his lips.

They heard Dawson's footsteps. They moved apart and Vonnie set her helmet on her collar locks, busying herself with it to obscure her flushed cheeks.

One more reason to shove him out the air lock, she thought happily. *I wanna jump Ben.*

"Neither of you has signed into your displays?" Dawson asked. He wore his helmet, which he aimed at them. Then he realized what they'd been doing. His cheeks reddened and he went to his station.

It was rare for the old coot to look shaken. Vonnie stalked after him while he was rattled. "Why did you drive here?" she said, but he ignored her.

He reactivated his display, enlarging the imagery to accommodate the bulky fingers of his gloves. "This is Dawson," he said. "06 is secure."

"Roger that," Koebsch said.

"Von, go to your station," Dawson said, uncomfortable with her closeness.

Peering over his shoulder, Vonnie saw most of the ESA and FNEE personnel on the group feed. A few were hidden by privacy screens. Tavares and a Brazilian lieutenant were missing completely. So was one of Vonnie's friends. There was a blank spot where Henri should have been.

"Dawson, why did you drive across camp?" she asked. "What did you do?"

"Go to your station. We're under alert."

I think you caused this emergency, she thought. *How?*

He was too cunning to leave evidence among his mem files or preferences. She crowded him anyway, studying his display as he examined their maps.

Far below, the sunfish had stopped 4.1 kilometers down, allowing ESA mecha to triangulate their position. Seismography indicated new digging. The tribe was also abnormally loud. They screamed against an ancient layer of ice, using it to conduct their voices throughout the area.

Preliminary translations from O'Neal read: **We are breaching the ice. Be ready. We are a Top Clan breaching the ice.**

"Oh shit," Ben said.

"They're warning us," Dawson said. "Administrator Koebsch, are you following our transcripts? We're also tracking two other tribes to the south and west."

"Yes," Koebsch said. "Wait."

"It looks like Top Clan Eight-Six is warning the other tribes, not us," Vonnie suggested.

O'Neal frowned and said, "It's probably both. They're using that solid mass to project their voices as far as possible."

"The other tribes are moving away from our camp, not joining an attack," Ben said.

"Correct me if I'm wrong, but sunfish typically run *toward* a fight," Dawson said. "Combat with us or our mecha would offer the chance to scavenge food and metal. That they've fled suggests an imminent large-scale disaster."

"Wait," Koebsch said.

He's not listening to us, Vonnie realized. Koebsch was staring at something on the group feed. She tried to mirror his gaze.

Then she saw what was holding his attention, and her voice raised in alarm.

"We have three people outside!" she said.

Despite the danger, three members of the combined crews had hurried onto the ice. Vonnie identified their suit beacons on the north side of camp.

They weren't in pressure suits like hers. They wore armor. One had exited Lander 04 — Henri — in an ESA scout suit designed for construction and survivability in hostile environments. Two had hurried from the Brazilians' main hab module — Tavares and her lieutenant — in FNEE suits which were heavier, slower, and intended for combat.

They'd gathered at a FNEE maintenance shed. What was inside it? Hand weapons? Why bother? After losing several mecha during their battle with the tribes, the Brazilians had built five new gun platforms with 20mm gatlings and STAT missile launchers. Their war machines patrolled the surface and the nearest catacombs, and for what?

Mecha were useless against geysers. Marching their guns in circles was another example of applying human perspectives to Europa's three-dimensional environment.

Nevertheless, Vonnie had briefly supported the show of force. The sunfish needed to count their resources and the firepower implied. Then she'd urged her leaders on Earth to put the mecha on standby. Maintaining their truce with Top Clan Eight-Six required calm and quiet. But the politicians didn't like quiet. They liked making bold pronouncements about protecting their astronauts and working in cooperation with their courageous allies from Brazil.

Some of them want to provoke the tribes, she reminded herself. It was a sinister thought and not a new one, although she still had trouble believing it.

You bastards. You want to fight.

She quit hovering at Dawson's shoulder and walked into her display. As a pilot, her role was to link to Lander 05's controls if she wasn't physically inside, but Ash had already initiated preflight checks on both landers. That left Vonnie free to investigate the FNEE shed.

Its data/comm channels were restricted.

"Shit," Vonnie said. "Koebsch, tell me what's going on. We can't take off with Henri outside."

Koebsch didn't take the bait. He was talking with someone behind a privacy screen. Vonnie couldn't hear their conversation, but he glanced at her and cut his hand at his throat, signaling for her to shut up.

She called Ash and Harmeet instead.

Ash blocked the call.

Harmeet answered from a showphone in 02 in B Lab, the genetics lab. Her matronly brown face was pale inside her helmet. "Von, I'm scared," she said. "We don't have enough landers to lift everyone."

"Why is Henri outside?"

"I don't know. Isn't he connecting new safety lines?"

"Our mecha can run the lines. Henri met two FNEE soldiers in their shed."

"I don't know. I don't know." Harmeet's eyebrows crinkled. "I need to hurry. I'm securing our gear in case there's a blowout."

"It won't come to that."

From her expression, Harmeet thought otherwise. "God bless," she said. Then she signed off, leaving Vonnie to worry at the benediction.

Harmeet Johal was a genesmith, an educated woman who'd spent most of her fifty years using structural mass spectrometers and nanotech to identify and recombine the microscopic building blocks of life. She'd been short-listed for the Nobel Prize in 2106 for stimulating prenatal neurogenesis in test subject chimpanzee fetuses.

She was also a devout Christian who believed God had His reasons for His mysteries, which people — and now sunfish — were meant to unveil.

Harmeet was intensely curious, giving and kind. She was also fatalistic. She could often predict her results or the decisions made on Earth without being able to explain why. Vonnie thought Harmeet's premonitions stemmed from her intelligence, not her faith — but to Harmeet, each life was a part of God's plan. She thought everything was predestined.

Sometimes she's the stupidest genius I know, and that includes Dawson, Vonnie thought, struggling with her disappointment. She'd called Harmeet for advice. *But I don't believe her. I won't. It's not inevitable for us and the sunfish to kill each other.*

She raised a new privacy screen on her display so Dawson couldn't hear. Then she connected with Ben, who stood behind her. "I don't like where this is going," she said.

"It's not pretty."

"Do you have anything we can use?" she asked.

"Maybe. Look at this."

Ben was their planetary sciences expert as well as the lead biologist. He'd developed sims of potential collapses. There were several rock islands and a liquid sea suspended nearby in the ice, which implied volcanic activity in the mountains further down. But were the volcanoes extinct or simmering or active? Simmering, he'd theorized. The rocks were hundreds of years old, and the local debris didn't appear to have been replenished by new eruptions. The sea had gradually frozen in layers, thickest on top, thinner on the bottom.

"The tribe went in the wrong direction if they want to flood us," he said. "They might be going for a magma seam. I can't tell. They're too far below."

"They're running away."

"But their sonar calls are territorial. They're announcing a confrontation. I'm sorry, Von."

Me too, she thought, feeling guilty for what she would say next. Ben was naturally rebellious. He loved her because she was a firebrand. If he'd been the type who wanted an office job, two kids and a dog, he wouldn't have come to Europa, but she worried that he'd end his career by conspiring with her.

"We've been tricked," she said.

Ben snorted. "Dawson was so nice when we suited up, I almost puked. That's how he acts when he gets what he wants. He's gracious in victory."

"Why do you think Henri went outside? Is he arming a weapons system or trading codes with the FNEE?"

"What kind of system?"

"Ben, I'm guessing. Why else would they meet in person?"

"Yeah. Fuck." Ben skimmed through his group feed as if weighing who was present and who wasn't.

A few tasks were never given to machines — not after the war. Otherwise Earth wouldn't have sent men and women into space. Mecha were less expensive. In many ways, machines were also more reliable. Machines didn't get excited or angry or sad, although they could be subverted.

Ultimately, the same fault existed in human beings. For civilian organizations like the ESA, the difficulty lay in hiring the best engineers and scientists without bringing in trojan horses. Decades of education were impossible to fake, but too many militaries and spy agencies wanted control over off-world missions. They swayed people with money or threats. They appealed to feelings of patriotism or injustice.

Henri Frerotte was a biologist like O'Neal and Ben. He genuinely shared their fascination with the sunfish. He'd helped Vonnie before, but, like Harmeet and Dawson, he was full of contradictions.

Weeks ago, Henri had revealed himself as a mole working for French national security. He'd taken part in forging the new ESA/FNEE alliance to open a divide between Brazil and China. He placed Earth politics above the welfare of any sunfish, and Vonnie couldn't hate him for it even if she disagreed.

She supposed she'd developed her own contradictions. She was an engineer, good with machines and math. For most of her life, she'd been lousy at listening to her heart. Dealing with the sunfish had made her more intuitive like Harmeet.

Henri doesn't realize he's being used, she thought. *Either that or he sees no choice. Our crew has been manipulated by some extraordinarily powerful people.*

Maybe it's not too late to muck up their plans.

"Ben, I need a wingman," she said, and his answer was an amused drawl.

"Yep."

"Are you sharing your updates with Dawson and Koebsch?"

"Yep."

"Let's piggyback into their stations. I want to find out what they're doing before they do it."

"Hacking the command line sounds like the kind of thing that gets people thrown in jail," he said. It wasn't a complaint. He said it like a dare.

She considered joking back. *Maybe they'll lock us in the same room with nothing to do except make love.* But she didn't want to tease him anymore. He deserved better. He'd earned her devotion if she could learn how to give it.

He can teach me, she thought. *Business first.*

"Ash and I wrote CEW codes into our mecha before we merged our grid with Ribeiro's," she said. "I should be able to tap his feed. I can definitely open Dawson's station. You need to run interference for me with as much noise as you can generate."

Ben grinned. "Noise is my middle name," he said.

"I love you. Um." *Did I just say that out loud?* she thought. Her cheeks burned — but for once, Ben didn't parry with a wiseass remark.

"Let's go," he said casually.

She couldn't look at him, feeling shy excitement. *I should love him*, she thought. *And he loves me.*

They acted in concert not unlike her dances with Tom.

Ben generated ten new sims, choking the ESA datastreams. Vonnie laced segments of his files with her counter-electronic warfare codes. By now, Top Clan Eight-Six had penetrated the solid layer of ice, falling silent as they vanished beneath the ancient mass. It was a good moment for Ben to increase his mock-ups detailing the existence of new seas and mountains. "Koebsch, we can stand down," he said. "The sunfish are gone."

"Nonsense," Dawson said on the group feed.

"They're four point three klicks below us and two point two north of camp," Ben said.

Dawson shook his head. "At best, your sims are ranked at fifty percent accuracy. You can't say what's below that layer of ice, and we know the cavities in its underside are caused by steam or geysers, which correlate with ongoing volcanic activity."

"The layer acts like a shield," Ben said.

"They've tunneled through it at a thin point," Dawson said. "Look at your third sim. If they flood their hole, that layer may crack laterally. How many subsurface seas will spill in the collapse?"

"There's only one sea within a four kilometer radius."

"You've located two additional seas within five kilometers as well as several rivers and catacombs. Don't minimize the severity of our situation for her," Dawson said. He emphasized *her* with a patronizing tone.

"Got you," Vonnie murmured.

She'd hacked the telemetry from his jeep, identifying a submenu that didn't belong, not to a genesmith.

Like everyone, Dawson could access their listening posts and mecha. At 14:01:33 local time while he was driving from camp, he'd run a diagnostic on their spies, actively involving himself in their grid rather than leaving standard checks to the engineers. Of course he'd have an explanation. He'd laid the groundwork for it among his mem files.

I know what he'll say, she thought.

The sunfish had bioelectric sensing organs like sharks, although the sunfish were more sensitive. They were stronger. Dawson would claim his research implied they could also generate bioelectric fields, allowing them to jam the spies. He'd say he'd driven to Module 06 because he was concerned for her safety. Then he'd started this whole mess himself.

His diagnostic had included a command for ten spies to wriggle a few millimeters at the same time. The quake would have obscured a minor commotion from ESA sensors — not from the hyper-aware sunfish. If the tribe had abruptly detected ten spies near their home, it could explain why they'd fled.

But he isn't a programmer, she thought. *Maybe we can track his records to whoever designed the command for him.*

Is it one of us? The FNEE?

"Damn it," Ben said inside their privacy screen. "Von, we're in trouble."

"We might be okay," she said.

"Von—"

"I can prove Dawson caused the tribe to run. We'll tell our proxies and show the media. Then we need to stop the tribe from hurting anyone."

"We're past that," he said. "Look."

Vonnie lifted her gaze from her work and glanced at a new feed on her display. Her heart leapt in shock.

Ben had used her codes to access the datastreams from the FNEE maintenance shed, including a surveillance camera. The shed was packed with moderately damaged diggers and other mecha in need of repair. Standing among the machines were Henri Frerotte and the two FNEE soldiers. They'd carried an ESA storage container inside with them.

The four-by-two-by-one-meter box was identical to hundreds of containers attached to the exterior of their ship, the *Clermont*, differing only in its ID codes.

It did not hold food or lab gear.

From it, Henri had unloaded ten pony bombs. He'd armed five of the quarter-kiloton devices. Then he'd attached the warheads to five FNEE diggers.

The first bomb had been activated seven minutes ago.

In the floor of the shed was a hatch.

The FNEE lieutenant had keyed two codes into the hatch, opening it. Then the diggers had scurried into the fractures beneath the surface.

"They're invading," Ben said.

"No. My God." Vonnie swallowed hard. "They want to seal the ice forever."

6.

Dozens of political, military, and corporate groups sought to undercut the ESA at every step. They said dealing with the sunfish was too costly. They said Earth had no concern in the affairs of savage aliens.

Vonnie accepted that millions of people regarded the sunfish with greed or fear, but she was astonished that billions didn't care at all.

It was their indifference that allowed the bad guys to act against the tribes.

Ben explained the social equation like this: In some ways, ironically, humankind's success had been its undoing. Civilization had bred out the demand for the "nomad gene," and restlessness and imagination went hand in hand. So did imagination and empathy.

In the twenty-second century, with cheap energy and abundant genesmithed crops and fisheries, Earth's population had swelled to 9.3 billion. Most of them lived in comfort. Many couldn't see past their holo streams. What they adored were sex dramas and police dramas as evidenced by the sky-high ratings for repetitive stories about criminals, corrupt statesmen, top cops and hot females. Popular media had also cycled around to yet another infatuation with vampires — idealized gods who combined humankind's darkest tendencies with everyone's desire to hold onto their youth and health.

Europa was too strange for some people to comprehend. Worse, the ESA mission was physically static. The astronauts stay-ed inside their modules because sending them into the ice was suicide, but the public wanted eye candy. They wanted linear narratives and certain gratification, not open-ended scenarios with complex issues.

Vonnie knew there were smart, honest adults in the world. She heard from them on the net. Unfortunately, too many leaders scoffed at her moral compass. Instead of doing the right thing, they rationalized why they should do what was easiest or most profitable.

The most profitable path was to treat the sunfish like vermin. Earth's space-faring nations had grown rich on the ice. For eighteen years before life was discovered beneath the surface, they'd mined Europa for deuterium, supplying orbital stations and fusion ships throughout the solar system.

The mining hadn't stopped after First Contact. It couldn't. Earth's militaries stockpiled fuel and water to create tactical advantages over each other, and even the civilian agencies worried about the sustainability of their operations.

Vonnie recognized that they needed the ice. How much was too much and who owned it? Should they offer payment? Merely landing on Europa had disrupted the native culture. By providing tools and food, the ESA wanted to boost the prominence of Top Clan Eight-Six among the other tribes. They hoped to rebuild the sunfish empire — not because they were idealistic pansies — because peace would allow them to explore and mine Europa safely. But what if Eight-Six wasn't best suited to unite the barbaric tribes?

Asking such questions allowed her opponents to call her indecisive. They didn't have answers themselves, but they didn't want answers for the sunfish. Not asking questions didn't make them stronger than her. It made them smaller. They liked to preen by saying they were taking care of people, creating jobs, keeping their nations secure, all the usual smoke and mirrors to conceal the genocide they'd planned.

Our lives are so much easier than the lives of the sunfish, but nothing is ever enough, she thought. *Too many people only take and take. They think it's weak to give.*

I'll give them something.

"Koebsch, I have emergency data packets for you and our proxies," she said. "You need to see this." Glancing over her shoulder, she signaled Ben with one hand, counting down from five fingers, four, three...

Koebsch answered her on a private channel. "Von, your responsibility is piloting Lander 05."

"I'm not flying 05," she said.

His eyes were hectic. He was juggling several data/comm feeds. "Von, do it now," he said. "Protecting our crew comes first."

"There's no danger if you shut off Henri's bombs."

"You'll pilot 05 or I'll lock your station. Tony and Ash can take the landers."

"This crisis was faked! It's a setup. Dawson ran a bullshit diagnostic on our spies to scare the sunfish, and I can guess who authorized the bombs."

"We don't have time for..." Koebsch hesitated.

"Let me show you," she said.

"Not now. After we're in the air."

"By then it will be too late."

"Are you going to log into 05?" he asked.

"Berlin hid missile components on the *Clermont* for our defense, I get it," she said, trying to slow him down. "We're a long way from home, we're at odds with China, and we were still on the fence with Brazil when we left Earth. But you can't think it was a good idea to bring the warheads into camp. Did Henri or Ash surprise you with that storage container?"

Koebsch dropped his gaze. The gesture was almost like nodding his head.

He hates this as much as I do, but he's stuck, she thought. *They sent the missiles with us for good reason. The Chinese ship is a destroyer. It could force us to leave Europa. We needed the deterrents, but then it was too easy for the wrong people to misappropriate our weaponry.*

"How far down will the FNEE diggers carry our warheads before they detonate?" she asked. "Two klicks? Three? They'll also travel sideways. We have time to stop them."

"My orders are to get in the air before the sunfish open another geyser or a volcano," Koebsch said. "It doesn't matter who started it. You need to log into 05. Lift your hab module to Evac Point F."

"The detonations will cause blowouts and collapses for a hundred kilometers," she said. "That includes the NASA and PSSC camps. We'll make them evacuate, too, and this is the most inhabited area we've found." She touched her maps, highlighting every point of contact with abandoned ruins or living sunfish, eels, bugs, bacterial mats and fungi.

Koebsch couldn't stop himself from looking, his silent gaze flitting up and down.

Ten thousand years ago, E uropa's southern pole had been a vibrant world. From a ncient tunnels and carvings, they guessed the sunfish had once colonized hundreds of cubic kilometers of ice. Now the survivors existed within a few scattered pockets. The pole was a decaying oasis.

"Our bombs will sterilize it," she said. "We'll kill the tribes. Then the ice will freeze into a solid mass like a shell. Don't you see? They *want* a permanent barrier between us and whatever else is down there. Five warheads are a small price to pay to restart full-scale mining ops."

Koebsch said nothing.

Vonnie remembered Harmeet's premonition. The ESA flight-craft were designed to carry one module each. So was the FNEE shuttle. She said, "Even if we go, trying to evacuate is bad math. Two landers, three modules. Ribeiro has the same problem with one shuttle and two modules. It won't work."

"I..." Koebsch lowered his gaze again in shame. "We'll come back for Harmeet," he said.

"You'd leave her behind?"

"Our mecha can start pulling her module away. As soon as the rest of us are clear, we'll send a lander for her."

She knew how he would decide, Vonnie thought. *I can't believe it. Dawson caused this mess but Harmeet gets stuck holding the bag.*

I'll lift her to safety first, not us. I'm sorry, Ben. We can't abandon Harmeet while Dawson gets away.

Koebsch must have seen the discord in Vonnie's gaze. Even as she made her choice, he reached into his display. He locked her station, permitting her to hear and see their group feed but not to interact with their grid.

"Wait!" she shouted.

"Tony, you're piloting 05," Koebsch said. "Ash, are you ready with 04?"

"Yes, sir," Ash said.

"I want you to lift 01. Tony, grab 06. The FNEE shuttle can take their command module. Henri will ride out with our mecha. We'll fly back for Harmeet as soon as possible."

"Yes, sir."

"I can't let you do that," Vonnie blurted, sick with dread and guilt. She loathed working against her friends. Their leaders in Berlin might crucify her for insubordination, but the unprovoked slaughter of the tribes would be an atrocity.

She finally signaled Ben.

"*Jetzt,*" she said in German. *Now.*

Koebsch hadn't restricted Ben's station. Ben broadcast his sims on their public channels and to a specific group of AIs: the proxies.

Loading the ESA databanks with electronic ghosts had been Berlin's answer to the distance between Earth and Europa. NASA had received the same treatment from Washington. The FNEE had proxies, too, and it was common knowledge that the PSSC astronauts were closely ruled by their own watchdogs.

An artificial intelligence in all but name, a proxy should have been a violation of western laws prohibiting human-based AI personalities. As usual, the politicians had made exceptions for themselves, then for their underlings and supporters.

Each proxy was the result of a comprehensive interview with the VIP it represented. Establishing the base personality took hours on the VIP's part — but then copies could be made, augmented with specific directives, and transmitted anywhere in the system. They were a cheap way to maintain authority over sensitive missions. They were disposable. They were inhuman.

They examined Ben's data with AI speed, then interrupted Koebsch with questions and demands. Vonnie couldn't hear what the proxies were saying. They appeared on private channels inside Module 01. In the chaos, however, Koebsch forgot to remove himself from the group feed.

His response told her what was happening.

"Prime Minister Yoshinao, your outrage is valid and I share it," Koebsch said with stiff formality. "Yes. I apologize. President Manihuari, I want an explanation, too. Admiral Cornet has confirmed the telemetry is accurate."

He means the telemetry showing Dawson's command to the spies, she thought. *Now the proxies know what really happened, and some of them are furious.*

Will they order us to...?

"Stand down," Koebsch said on the group feed. "Tony, Ash, stand down. Don't lift off. Colonel Ribeiro, inform your men. I want everyone on high alert, but don't move the landers. All mecha hold position."

"Affirmative," Ribeiro said. His taut expression never changed. The man was like stone.

"Von, what did you do!?" Ash yelled.

"I'm saving lives," Vonnie said.

"Henri, get off the ice," Koebsch said. "With permission from Colonel Ribeiro, I'd like you to join the FNEE. Their hab modules are closest."

"Permission granted, of course," Ribeiro said as Henri added, "Roger that."

"We might only have a few minutes before our orders are rescinded and we evacuate," Koebsch said. "Harmeet, I need you to leave 02. Run. A jeep will bring you to Module 01."

"Thank you," Hameet gasped. "Thank you." Her round, dusky

face was terrified. Then she vanished from the group feed, briefly leaving a view of her lab before she remembered to switch to her helmet cam. Her breathing grew louder as she stumbled into 02's ready room and keyed the air lock.

"Colonel Ribeiro, join me on the command line," Koebsch said. "We may disarm our warheads."

"Affirmative," Ribeiro said. He and Koebsch vanished from the group feed, raising new privacy screens, which didn't stop Dawson from complaining.

"Administrator Koebsch, a delay now is asinine," Dawson said. "Our lives are at stake."

Vonnie bared her teeth at him — an elated grin — trying to recall the proxies' names she'd heard. Yoshinao was the Japanese prime minister. Manihuari was from Peru, an ally of Japan and an influential neighbor of Brazil. She didn't recognize the name Admiral Cornet, but she was glad to learn there was a military commander in the mix. Not all of the proxies were opposed to aiding the sunfish.

"Goddamn it, we can't wait for a geyser or a quake!" Ash yelled. She moved her hands across her display, and, on the group feed, the cameras in Lander 04 trembled as she initiated its fusion jets.

Alarm bars filled Ben's display. "Ash, you were ordered to stand down," he said.

"I won't!"

"The proxies are reconsidering our situation," he told her as Vonnie said, "They *should* reconsider. Ash, look at our sims. Don't let Dawson panic you."

"This is crazy," Ash hissed.

"No." Vonnie met her gaze on the group feed. "It's the most sane thing we can do."

Ashley Sierzenga was their youngest crew member. Twenty-four years old, she looked nineteen with her freckles and her slender, flat-chested body.

A month ago, for several days, she and Vonnie had been buddies. Ash wanted to be older. She was eager for the world to take her seriously. They'd developed a big sister little sister relationship, working side by side on maint or ROM projects, sharing late-night drinks, flirting together with Henri and Ben — but like Henri, Ash had an agenda.

The young woman worked for MI6. She was in Vonnie's debt because Vonnie had saved her life, but she was also a hard case who refused to disobey her handlers. If they'd said it was in Britain's interests to preserve the ESA's assets at any cost, Ash would fulfill her objectives.

Vonnie and Ash had had their falling out because of Ash's rigidity in acting as she was told. Ash was a spy first, an astronaut second, a free individual last of all. The pleasure she took in following orders was especially maddening because Vonnie shared her regard for duty and honor. They just didn't agree on what was honorable.

"Ash, look at our sims," Vonnie said. "Make up your own mind. Use your head."

The young woman growled at her. She didn't speak. She growled. But she dropped the power on Lander 04. Then she cut her audio and whispered something to O'Neal beside her, a few bitter words. She was going to be trouble.

Koebsch, we need a decision.

He was taking too long. From what Vonnie had heard, some of the proxies wanted peace. How many were actually on her side?

Yoshinao, Manihuari, Cornet, she thought. She left her station and stepped close to Ben, wrapping one arm around his waist. "Please," she said. "Can I access your display?"

"Here." Ben was remodeling their radar scans of the ice, but he took an instant to create a new window.

Vonnie used it to scroll through the proxies' org charts. She hardly knew them all. Berlin, like Washington and Tokyo, had agreed to copy its allies' proxies if they reciprocated. Hundreds of personalities were stored in Module 01 including representatives from smaller nations, science groups, conservationist groups and religious parties, most of them lesser AIs whose roles were to observe. They collated data. They made independent reports to Earth. It was the few Level I intelligences who guided Koebsch's day-to-day management, but a three-quarters majority might stall or overrule the top proxies.

She added fuel to the fire.

"This is Alexis Vonderach," she said on Ben's display. "I can prove who's culpable in the unlawful deployment of nuclear weapons. Do you think people want to see Europa destroyed like London or Nanjing? If you don't stop the bombing, I'll expose your involvement."

Ben clutched her wrist. "Von!" he said wildly. "What if they kill us to stop you?"

"They wouldn't. They can't."

"The top proxies must have the det codes. If they set off the bombs, they'll vaporize everyone in camp."

"The cost to replace us..."

"Once we were gone, they could do whatever they want. They could say the sunfish triggered the bombs somehow, blame the tribes and say they're the good guys."

Vonnie was already moving data through his station. As soon as she finished, she called the proxies again. "My files have been transmitted to the *Clermont*," she said. "In thirty seconds, if I don't provide another command, it will send those files to Earth. You'll go to jail."

"Everybody listen up," Koebsch said on the group feed. "I think everyone should see this."

He patched them into a real-time account of the proxies' standings. Hundreds were undecided or caught in debates, but dozens of votes had been cast — and with inhuman efficiency, the proxies committed. Some abstained. Some demanded evacuation and self-defense. Yet the trend was clear.

More votes than not called for restraint.

"This is absurd," Dawson muttered as Ash said, "Sir, what about the sunfish? We can't just sit here."

"We'll keep our warheads in the catacombs as a fail-safe and move everyone into the landers," Koebsch said. "Then we'll make reparations to the tribe if we can."

"That sim recording the telemetry from my jeep is a fraud," Dawson said. "Our spies adjusted their positions *after* the sunfish detected our grid and began to disable the spies' sensors with organic EMPs."

"He's lying," Vonnie said.

"We'll let Earth analyze our data," Koebsch said as he removed the Class 1 alert from the group feed.

"My reputation—!" Dawson began.

"Not now," Koebsch said.

"Administrator, you cannot underestimate the value of my good name."

"We'll wait for further analysis," Koebsch said firmly. "Stand down. Stand down."

Vonnie wanted to kiss Ben. She settled for thumping her helmet against his helmet and beaming at him. "Yes!" she celebrated.

"Look who sided with us," Ben said.

She nodded. Counting their supporters among the proxies was a study in global politics, and she recorded their names and nationalities. With the right help, could she consolidate them into a permanent voting bloc?

Venezuela. Malaysia. Israel. Ukraine. The influence they'd been permitted was tiny, which might have encouraged them to act as a collective thorn in the side of Earth's most powerful nations. Countries without spaceflight, like Peru, could afford to demand peace. Japan owned five orbital factories and often partnered with the Americans in space, but after losing more cities during another World War, their people held their integrity in higher regard than profits.

Admiral Joost Cornet was a surprise ally. Skimming his file, Vonnie saw why he'd taken her side. Originally from the Netherlands, the real Cornet lived in Berlin, where he served with EUSD, European Union Space Defense, a federal arm of their military. He had nationalist leanings, however. His politics were "orange." That meant he supported the rights of his country to maintain local control and traditions while loyally serving the union.

He must think the tribes deserve local control, too, she thought. *Good for him.*

Other supporters might have seemed less likely. Weeks ago, seeking common ground, Vonnie had tried to align herself with a consortium she'd first regarded as an enemy: the gene corps.

Earth's bio industries wanted DNA. The sunfish had more intriguing traits than their odd hemoglobin. The sunfish were also resistant to cold and radiation, two abilities of supreme importance in space. Perhaps more impressive, genesmiths like Dawson believed they could improve human longevity treatments based on sunfish metabolic tricks.

Diverse samples and testing meant sustained contact. Vonnie had urged the gene corps to befriend the sunfish because forging treaties would cost less than defending themselves against never-ending guerrilla warfare.

Many of the gene corps had sided with her. One exception was LifeNova. Dawson was in LifeNova's pocket. He had accepted payments from them, and their board did not share Vonnie's opinion that sustained contact with the tribes was desirable.

From the beginning, mecha from all four Earth agencies had stolen blood and tissue samples from the sunfish. Intact corpses had been excavated from the ice. Men like Dawson hoped for live specimens, too, but he seemed to have traded that prize for the chance to develop his samples without interference from do-gooders like Vonnie. LifeNova already had what they wanted, and their uncompromising view had made the rounds on several chat shows on the net: If the tribes were gone — if they'd been annihilated — who could argue against monetizing their remains?

Dawson acts like a gentleman to cover the fact that he's a borderline sociopath, she thought. *He never learned he's not the center of the universe. That's why he's so awkward with us. No one else is alive to him. We're just in the way.*

The spark of pity she felt was overcome by condemnation. She shut off her work on Ben's display. Then she stepped away from Ben and marched to the next station, where Dawson was bickering with Koebsch.

"Unacceptable!" Dawson said. "If we relocate to the landers, you must transfer my lab materials."

"I have other priorities," Koebsch said.

Dawson jabbed an index finger at him like a petulant old king. "Nothing is more critical than—"

"Stop it," Vonnie said. "I have you by the balls, so back off. Let us get things organized without more bullshit out of you."

Dawson sneered. "Administrator Koebsch, please. Her vulgarities are unprofessional and lewd."

"I mean it," Vonnie said. "Back the fuck off. You took part in stealing weapons of mass destruction. A lot of people will look at that as a terrorist act. They'll send you home and lock you up."

Dawson chuckled at her. "Always the Joan Of Arc. Your evaluation of the matter is skewed to say the least."

"You bastard."

"You're the one with her mouth in the gutter and a head full of conspiracy theories. I believe our resident secret agents are responsible for offloading those the warheads from the *Clermont,* which was fortuitous, since our capacity to protect ourselves is feeble indeed. If anyone is convicted of misbehavior, it will be Henri and Ash."

"The command you gave our spies is what spooked the

sunfish! Why do you hate them so much?"

"Hate is a sophomoric word. I find them repugnant, but the same could be said for a black widow or a Sloane's viperfish. I'm not emotionally invested. Why are you? Did your parents withhold affection when you were a child?"

Boiling, she said, "That's funny. I've been thinking the same thing about you."

"Both of you, stop," Koebsch said. "We don't—"

"Heads up!" Ben yelled. "I have new radar signals in the ice. The sunfish are coming back."

Dawson's face lost its color. Vonnie's mood soared, although she couldn't deny that she felt some apprehension herself. "Where?" she asked.

"They're above the layer where they disappeared. Range three point eight kilometers," Ben said.

Ash rejoined the group feed and posted sims from their other sensors — sonar, seismography, neutrino pulse. "Something's wrong with their formation," she said. Her eyes were grim. "Are you sure this is the same tribe?"

"Voice recognition shows Tom and Charlotte in the lead. There's Hans, Peter and Brigit," Ben said, identifying several members of the pack.

"Can you tell where they're going?" Vonnie asked. "Are they headed home?"

"They're coming straight at us," Ash said.

ESA EUROPA BASE
Revised 1 September 2113

Command_____.
Koebsch, Peter Günther

Engineering_____.
Gravino, Antionio Leonardo
Sierzenga, Ashley Nicole
Vonderach, Alexis Rose

Life Sciences_____.
Dawson, William George
Frerotte, Henri Charles
Johal, Harmeet
Metzler, Benjamin Todd
O'Neal, Dublin David

Koebsch	COMMAND - PSY - DATA/COMM
Dawson	GENE SMITH
Johal	GENE SMITH - MED - HAB
Frerotte	BIOLOGY - HAB - ASST. SUIT MAINT - ASST DATA/COMM
Metzler	BIOLOGY - PLANETARY - ASST. ROM
O'Neal	LINGUISTICS - BIOLOGY - ECOLOGY - ASST. ROM
Sierzenga	PILOT - NAV - MED - DATA/COMM - CYBERNETICS
Vonderach	PILOT - NAV - MAINT - MED - ROM
Gravino	ENGINEERING - PILOT - MED - HAB - DATA/COMM

Mission Control:
ESOC – Darmstat

Craft:
Deep Space *Intruder*-class *Clermont*
Deep Space Reconnaissance *Marcuse*

Support:
DSSC Hab Modules (2), ROM-12 Lander Flightcraft (2)
ROM-4 APAQS Modules (1), ROM-12 ATMP Vehicles (3), ROM-12 Rovers (7),
ROM-12 GP Mecha (14), ROM-12 Beacons (29), ROM-12 MMPSA (2)
ROM-12 Rovers (1), ROM-12 MMPSA (3), ROM-12 MMPSA (14) // Japan
ROM-12 GP Mecha (9), ROM-6 Beacons (4) // United States of America
ROM-6 GP Mecha (1) // Australia

Constructed On-Site:
DSSC Hab Module 06
Submodule 07 Exploratory
ROM-12 "Doppelganger" Probes (10)
ROM-12 MMPSA (12), ROM-12 Beacons (5)

*** Intercept *** Eyes Only *** Intercept *** Eyes Only *** Intercept ***

Força Nacional de Exploração do Espaço
Missão 298   30 De junho de 2113

Personnel   .
Colonel Ribeiro
Major Correa
Captain Alvaréz
Captain Araújo
Lieutenant Santos
Lieutenant Carvalho
Lieutenant Pereira
Sergeant Tavares

Ribeiro	COMMAND - NAV - ROM - ASST. ENGINEERING
Correa	COMMAND - MED - PSY - HAB - ASST. ENGINEERING
Alvaréz	PILOT - WEAPONS - MED - HAB
Araújo	PILOT - WEAPONS - ASST. ROM - ASST. MED
Santos	ROM - ENGINEERING - BIOLOGY
Carvalho	ROM - NAV - TECH/COMM - BIOLOGY
Pereira	ROM - WEAPONS - ASST. NAV - ASST. PILOT
Taraves	TECH/COMM - NAV - MED - HAB - ASST. ROM

Mission Control:
Alcântara

Craft:
FNEE *Leopard*-class *M4*

Support:
ROM-4 Hab Modules (2), ROM-6 Orbital Shuttle (1)
ROM-2 APAQS Modules (3), ROM-4 Rovers (5),ROM-4 AP Mecha (15),
ROM-6 SD Mecha (10), ROM-4 Sentries (10), ROM-2 Beacons (15)

7.

"Koebsch, I need my station," Vonnie said.

"Yes. Go," he said.

Vonnie ran from Dawson to her display, where Koebsch restored full access. The others were absorbed with tracking the sunfish. Vonnie paged through their datastreams to find Harmeet, then located her in Module 01.

Good. She's not alone. I don't think the sunfish will attack, but if they do...

Dawson had recovered his superior air. He raised his nose at Vonnie and said, "Will you be sauntering down to your private little rendezvous to meet them?"

Vonnie flashed him a wolfish grin, hoping he couldn't see her pulse in her throat. "That's a great idea," she said.

"Nobody leaves their station," Koebsch said.

Ash conspicuously began another preflight check on Lander 04. "What are your orders, sir?" she asked.

Koebsch glanced at her. "Our orders are unchanged. Stand down."

"Sir, this isn't the same tribe," Ash said.

"She's right." Ben opened a new analysis on the group feed. "I count more sunfish than before. Forty. Fifty. Seventy."

"They found another group," Vonnie said.

"They found *reinforcements*," Dawson corrected her.

"We encouraged them to introduce us to new tribes. What if they're doing what we asked?" Vonnie said, but her pulse continued to rise with the increasing tension among her friends.

"They're in two clusters of different sizes, a lead element of sixteen and a main group of fifty-eight," Ash said. "Range three point one kilometers. The lead element is moving fast. I track 'em at thirty kilometers an hour. At that pace, even with the twists and turns in the catacombs, they'll reach the FNEE diggers in five minutes. They're sprinting."

"They're using their burst speed," Dawson said. "It's an indication of attack. They want to catch us off-guard. Koebsch, we *must* fire our warheads!"

"Look where the diggers are!" Vonnie said as Ben explained, "The bombs are too close, Dawson. Open your eyes. If we detonate, we'll get caught in the blast."

"I concur," Ribeiro said. "Administrator Koebsch, a single warhead is the solution. Number four. It's the deepest and the farthest north. It will blunt the sunfish attack and divert them away from our position."

"What about us?" Koebsch asked.

"Moderate quakes," Ribeiro said. "My calculations set our survivability at ninety-eight percent."

"That's optimistic," Ben said.

"The most severe damage will be localized beyond our north perimeter," Ribeiro said. "The FNEE modules are most endangered. My officers accept the risk."

"Koebsch, his numbers are wrong," Ben said. "The catacombs are limited in the area he's talking about. There aren't a lot of open spaces to buffer the shock wave. The path of least resistance is *up*. It'll rip open the surface before it causes a huge collapse. If the shrapnel doesn't kill us, the cave-ins will."

"My calculations are correct," Ribeiro said.

Koebsch was shouting at the proxies behind a privacy screen. In the abrupt silence, Harmeet signed onto the group feed from Module 01, her dark bangs curled with sweat inside her helmet. But her eyes were clear. If she'd panicked while she rushed across camp from 02, that lonely terror was gone now.

She addressed the crew in her cool, understated manner. "It's irresponsible to kill the sunfish before we know what they want," she said. "In any case, they can't hurt us directly. Breaching the surface would expose them to vacuum."

"They can climb from 07 into 06," Dawson said. "They'll pour in here like—"

"The hatches are sealed," Ben said scornfully.

"They could break through the access tube."

"It's ten millimeter thick steel with another hatch on top, plus a blast door in the entry room."

Dawson wasn't listening. He fidgeted, turning to stare at the corridor as if he'd imagined noises behind them. "Koebsch, do something!" he said.

"The choice to wait and see is doing something," Harmeet said. She was serene, even motherly.

"The lead element of sunfish will pass the FNEE diggers and our warheads in two minutes," Ash said. Her voice was strained like Dawson's.

"Koebsch, we have other options," Vonnie said.

"We should evacuate!"

"I mean Lam," Vonnie said.

"Why would—?"

"Call Lam. Call him now."

"We haven't heard from Lam in weeks," Ash said as Koebsch

dropped his privacy screen. "Colonel Ribeiro, your team has the most sensors on our northern perimeter," he said. "Please boost our signals to Probe 114. Ash, I want the 114 CEW codes you designed immediately."

"Sir, one hundred seconds to intercept," Ash said.

"Roger that. Transmit your CEW codes."

"Transmitting now."

"Colonel Ribeiro, report."

Ribeiro showed some feeling at last. He let indignation creep into his tone. "Of course we are relaying your codes at maximum gain."

"Eighty seconds," Ash said.

Time slowed to crawl as Vonnie held her breath, staring at her display. She wanted to see a new mecha appear on their grid — an old mecha to be more precise.

Probe 114 had gone missing eleven hours after the ESA formalized their treaty with Top Clan Eight-Six. Before it vanished, however, 114 had been instrumental in developing the agreements between the two species. 114 had recorded the sunfish while they believed they were unobserved. It had mapped the tribe's home, their hunting grounds, and the neutral regions between their colony and the territories of other tribes.

Probe 114 was also sentient. It carried the mem files of a Chinese astronaut named Choh Lam, although his mind had been fragmented, repaired, fragmented, then repaired again with insufficient memory in the darkness of the frozen sky.

Originally a Level II intelligence, many of Lam's cognitive scores had tested at Level I after Vonnie fed him corrective sequences. Like a sunfish, Lam was capable of fluid mental leaps — and yet in other regards such as mission fidelity, he'd tested as low as Level IV.

He was deranged.

Human thinking had evolved for the human body and vision and light. All of that had been taken from him. He no longer had two arms, two legs, a head or eyes or even a mouth in the normal description of the word.

The mecha he inhabited, Probe 114, was shaped like a sunfish. Vonnie and the other engineers had designed several of these doppelgängers to approach the tribes. Each probe had an alumalloy frame sheathed in synthetic skin with pedicellaria beneath their arms, a functioning beak, the appearance of gills, a genital slit and tiny reserves of saliva and blood.

Within his new body, Lam also had mechanical lungs. He could inhale and exhale convincingly. He was stronger than any sunfish and weighed ten kilos more than an equivalent-sized male due to his metal innards, which included a power plant, sonar, X-ray and data/comm. His hidden senses and his overt strength made him a supreme hunter. Such traits were esteemed by the sunfish, but he could not generate pheromones or sperm, so the matriarchs had initially regarded him a deviant.

He hadn't contacted the ESA for three weeks. They thought he'd wandered off or he'd been destroyed because their other probes had been smashed when he disappeared. Then during her conversations with Tom, Vonnie had learned that Lam was still with the tribe.

His silence unsettled her more than the idea that he'd been crushed by a rock slide or ripped apart in a fight. What was he doing down there? How could he ignore their broadcasts? Had he asked the sunfish to destroy their other probes?

They'd tracked him as often as possible. It helped that he was sixty percent metal, but they couldn't always penetrate the rock islands or the seas — and when they had been able to study him, he'd acted like a sunfish.

He seemed to have returned to the feral state in which he'd first joined the tribe. Tom described Lam as a leader now, a favored companion of the matriarchs, although his status was hindered by his sterility.

In other ways, his artificial nature had boosted his prestige. When he'd revealed himself as a human construct, Lam had disfigured one of his arms, peeling off his skin to expose the alumalloy beneath. The flesh at the base of this limb had healed in an ugly ring of scar tissue. Tom had sung about its glorious feel and taste.

Lam's metal arm was an emblem of power to the lesser males and a challenge to the matriarchs. He deferred to them, adding his might to their leadership, but he was a wild card.

He was the final piece of the ESA puzzle. His presence among Top Clan Eight-Six was why Vonnie had wanted to call Sergeant Tavares when the tribe fled. As the sunfish passed beneath the FNEE relays, Vonnie had hoped to hit Lam with a slavecast. A close-range beam might have reactivated his data/comm systems, which he'd turned off when he'd abandoned everything above the ice.

Will he — can he — help us? she wondered.

"Sir, no response to our CEW codes," Ash said. "Fifty seconds to intercept."

"Prepare for evac," Koebsch said.

"Hold on." O'Neal posted a new sim on the group feed. "I've been differentiating among their sonar calls. Most of the sunfish are the larger breed."

Vonnie's eyes widened. "Are they chasing the smaller sunfish?" she asked.

"Definitely not," O'Neal said. "The two breeds are intermingled. There are larger and smaller sunfish together in the lead element and in the main pack."

"I confirm Ash's count," Ben said. "Sixteen in front, fifty-eight behind. Lam is with the lead element."

He pinpointed one shape among the sunfish, a dense metal signature unlike the others' flesh and blood. The metal shape thrashed among its companions, who tumbled up through the catacombs in a berserker cloud.

"Both groups are biting and flailing at each other, but the violence is universal," Ben said. "They're all doing it."

"What the hell does that mean?" Koebsch asked.

"They're inciting each other to attack," Dawson said.

Vonnie shook her head. "No, they're not. We saw the same bonding ritual when the survivors of Top Clan Two-Four merged with Eight-Six. They're becoming a single tribe. The sunfish in the lead element are their scouts. The main pack consists of warriors and matriarchs."

"The different breeds don't work together," Dawson said. "They're natural enemies."

"Can you translate their calls?" Vonnie asked.

"It's inconclusive," O'Neal said. "Aggression. Conquest. They're warning other tribes to stay out of their way."

"They always threaten other tribes."

"Five seconds to intercept," Ash said. Her countdown had reached the final mark.

"I am arming Warhead Number Four," Ribeiro said, and Vonnie shouted: "Koebsch, don't let him fire! We asked Top Clan Eight-Six to introduce us to more sunfish!"

"Weapons tight," Koebsch said. "Do not fire."

"Sir, I'm... picking up a signal," Ash said reluctantly. "It's encrypted. It has Von's ID in the recognition codes."

"It's Lam. It has to be."

"Answer the signal," Koebsch said.

"Yes, sir," Ash said. "The sunfish are past the FNEE diggers, sir. I'm beginning a new countdown. They'll reach the hollows beneath our camp in two minutes."

Koebsch was overwhelmed with the proxies and a private channel to Ribeiro. Even so, he asked, "What can I do?"

"Transmitting CEW codes now," Ash said. "I'm using Von's ID, and I've realigned our mecha to act as a directional composite. He should be able to hear us loud and clear."

"Why don't we see a response?"

"I don't know. Ninety seconds."

"He may be damaged," Vonnie suggested as Ben said, "The lead element is splitting in half."

"They're coming toward Submodule 07!" Dawson cried.

"Affirmative," Ash said. "Eight of them are moving toward camp, eight toward Submodule 07. Contact in eighty seconds."

As the sunfish darted laterally through the ice, Dawson yelled, "Lam is strong enough to tear through the access tube! Good Lord, Koebsch! Fire!"

"Those bombs won't do any good now," Ben said.

"We can send our mecha into combat," Ribeiro said. "They are outnumbered, but they will make the tribe think twice."

"Do it! Protect us!"

The pressure on Koebsch was immense. Would he order the mecha to fight or tell his pilots to evacuate?

Thrumming with adrenaline, Vonnie bit her lip and drew blood, barely noticing the sting as she paged through their sims for any proof of the tribe's intentions. Too late. Koebsch tipped his head at Ribeiro and said, "We should have had a response if Lam is on our side. Tell the mecha—"

"Sir, I'm receiving an open broadcast," Ash said.

Vonnie wasn't sure what she expected. The high-pitched screeches of a sunfish? Garbled data? Koebsch had prepared their grid to repel the subversive assaults of a hostile AI, but when Ash punched a key on her display, they heard English in a calm male voice:

—This is Choh Lam on channels one through eight. I can feel your radar, so you've confirmed I'm with the tribe. Let me speak to Von.

"Ash, tell him you are Vonnie," Koebsch said. "Ask him what they're doing."

"I can talk to him!" Vonnie said.

"No. Our module has better resources." Koebsch gestured for Ash to proceed.

"Lam, it's Von," Ash said, using a simple electronic mask. It lowered her voice. She sounded like Vonnie as she asked, "Are we under attack? What is the tribe's objective?"

His reply was gibberish, although his tone remained un- naturally calm:

—Christmas shell what if music women.

On the group feed, everyone stared at each other. "He's dysfunctional," Koebsch said as Dawson cried, "The sunfish are almost here!"

"Try again," Koebsch said. "When he answers, I want a brute force override. We might be able to turn him against them if necessary. Hit him with everything we've got."

"Yes, sir," Ash said. "Lam, this is Von. Do you copy? Please acknowledge."

Silence.

"Lam? Are you there?" Ash scowled and turned to Koebsch. "Sir, no response."

"Radar shows him leaping among the other sunfish with a specific pattern of arm movements," O'Neal said. "Some of them are repeating it. I'll have a translation soon."

"Tell us what you can," Koebsch said, and O'Neal posted his sims in a flurry of piecemeal words:

LAM: Four / Two / Four / Two.

ALL SUNFISH: We are *<indicating great size>*

LAM: Louder / Closer.

ALL SUNFISH: *<shrieking>* We are four!

"It looks like more boasting and cruelty. It's always boasting and cruelty," Dawson said in a faint voice until Ben cut him off.

"You keep acting like they're you," Ben said. "They're not. They don't think like human beings."

"Their song is full of threat displays!"

"The two breeds are new to each other," O'Neal said. "They're still integrating. That makes them vulnerable as a tribe, so they're scaring off their enemies."

"What if we are their enemy?" Ribeiro's gaze burned with frustration as he spoke from his command module. "Eight sunfish from the lead element have reached our camp. They are swarming the mecha beneath us. They have knocked three diggers and a beacon to the ground."

"Sir, the rest of their lead element has entered the cavern with Submodule 07," Ash said. "We lost two relays and a listening post. They tore 'em apart."

"If the sunfish cause a blowout..." Dawson said.

"They won't," Ben said.

"They've used suicides before."

"A few males sacrificed themselves to preserve the tribe," Ben said. "That's their way. But they wouldn't bring seventy individuals to breach the surface. You're not worth that many lives, old man."

Vonnie managed a bleak smile. More than ever, she appreciated Ben's passion and insight. She wanted to join him in ridiculing Dawson, trying to defuse the moment, but most of her attention was focused on a last-ditch analysis of Lam's broadcasts. She knew what his strange words meant. She also worried at his tone. He hadn't sounded like a lonely human being or a conflicted AI. In fact, he'd demonstrated the total self-assurance of a sunfish.

Koebsch is right, she thought. *As much as I'd like to believe otherwise, Lam is dangerous.*

She'd dealt with him twice before in crisis situations. Each time, he'd been a cunning opponent. First he'd been killed beneath the ice — the real him, a scrupulous man who'd loved Europa for its secrets.

Vonnie had resurrected Lam's personality and intelligence from his mem files. Blinded by the hideous wounds in her face, she'd needed an AI to lead her through the catacombs. Unfortunately, Lam had tried to assume control of her scout suit, acting more like a virus than a true AI. Her bloody fights against the sunfish had occurred simultaneously with her quiet battles to outwit him.

In the end, she'd won, restoring a good portion of his mind. Lam had saved her life, but Koebsch had ordered him erased. If the ESA was caught using the ghost of a Chinese astronaut, the scandal could cause new political pressures on Earth or military posturing on Europa.

We've been enemies too many times, Vonnie thought as she finished her data analysis. *He was a great friend. Now he's not human anymore. I don't know what he is. Machine? Sunfish?*

"Administrator Koebsch, I request permission to protect my team!" Ribeiro said. "The lead element has destroyed our mecha. They are clawing at the ice."

"We're seeing the same thing around Submodule 07!" Dawson said. "Most of our spies have been wiped out! The listening post is disabled! The sunfish are excavating behind 07 or hammering on the access and cargo tubes!"

"The main group will arrive in sixty seconds," Ash said. "Twelve of them peeled away. They're going toward 07. The rest are approaching camp. We're about to have fifty-four sunfish below the FNEE hab modules."

Ribeiro glared at Koebsch on the group feed. "My officers need time to bring new diggers and gun platforms into position," he said. "If we choose to defend ourselves, we must act."

"Begin your preparations," Koebsch said.

"Stop," Vonnie said. "Let me talk to Lam."

"It's no good, Von. He won't answer."

"He isn't stupid. Even with a mask, Ash doesn't sound like me. She talks faster and she said 'objectives' when I'd say 'What do they want?'"

"You think he knew it was her?"

"He knew it wasn't me. That gibberish was a test."

Koebsch nodded. "I got some of it," he said. "Christmas Bauman was the American with your crew. She and Lam died when he tagged a shell in the ice."

"That's right. 'What if music women' were more prompts for me. He's suspicious, and I can't blame him."

"Here they come," Ash said.

Beneath the ESA/FNEE camp, a billowing wave of eight-armed bodies filled the ice. A smaller, similar bunch joined Lam around Submodule 07.

"They're screaming at maximum volume," O'Neal said. "The separate groups are communicating with each other. They're synchronizing. Radar shows the same pattern of arm movements in every sunfish."

"That's unlikely," Harmeet said. "Their pedicellaria and arm displays can't be conveyed except in close proximity."

"They're doing it anyway," O'Neal said. "I'm tracking the same message over and over. 'Four two, four two.' Christ. Listen to our sonar."

I can feel it, Vonnie thought.

Their song was a malevolent buzzing. The floor quivered and her bones hummed. Vonnie felt transfixed until Ash said, "They look like a pile of fucking snakes."

Vonnie glanced at the rest of their crews. Finding revulsion in

Dawson and Ribeiro wasn't a surprise, but Tony looked skittish, which was discouraging. Even Harmeet's round, motherly face was wrought with stress.

The sunfish raged at the ice.

"They're working themselves into some kind of frenzy," O'Neal said. "It's like a colony's affirmation ritual, but there are new undertones."

"We need to decide what it means," Koebsch said.

O'Neal spread his hands. "I don't know. An affirmation ritual builds to a climax. This song, this dance... they're sustaining it."

"Our mecha are positioned at the air lock," Ribeiro said.

"Don't you dare crash in there and start shooting," Vonnie said. "Koebsch, I can talk to Lam!"

"Let her do it," Ben said. "Ribeiro is misreading their behavior. The sunfish aren't trying to bring down the cavern walls. They're searching for more beacons and spies, and the FNEE diggers weren't destroyed. They were crippled. The sunfish only hurt 'em."

"They did more than that," Ash said. "They broke the diggers' legs and eyes."

"A sunfish would heal from similar wounds, and it's normal for them to treat newcomers roughly," Ben said. "We should have told our mecha to resist. The sunfish wouldn't expect anyone to accept a beating. They're probably confused. They might be angry. They wanted a dialogue."

"They're waiting for us to greet them," Vonnie said.

"A few of them have stopped screaming," O'Neal said. "Lam is pounding his metal arm against 07. He's using it like a drum. Their tempo is increasing."

"He's banging on the hatch," Ash said.

"Shit." Koebsch looked at Vonnie. "Call him."

She opened a public channel on her display and cleared her throat. She wanted to sound brave, even cavalier. How much of her anxiety was due to the bone-ringing sonar from the tribe? "Lam, it's me," she said. "There are some extremely nervous people up here who can't wait to use their big guns. Tell me what's going on."

—*Bajonette we embraced just like them.*

The emotions his words evoked were bittersweet. She would have liked to remember their best experiences, not their worst, but she shared his mistrust. The gulf between them had grown too wide. In fact, she wasn't sure what he meant by *just like them*, although she recognized his other clues.

"That was Ash on the radio before," she said. "Now it's really me." To prove herself, she responded to his code words. She said, "I hugged you before we entered the tunnel for the first time. The last time. Then I tried to kill you with emergency order *Bajonette*."

His answer was swift. —*Switch to Encryption I.*

"Switching now," she said. She keyed new codes on her display, but Koebsch said, "You can't let him isolate your feed. He could hack your station."

"He wants to make sure we don't hack into him," she said. "Otherwise he won't talk. What's the risk? Cut me out of the group feed. If it's a trap, we might lose one station. But if he can help us, this is our chance."

"I have early warning alerts from 07," Ash said. "Lam is beginning to affect the pressure seals on the hatch."

"We have a bigger problem," Ben said. "Their sonar is phys- ically affecting the ice. It's almost like a quake. If they don't stop..."

"Cracks are opening on the north perimeter!" Ribeiro shouted. "Our sensors register outgassing!"

He posted FNEE sims that overlaid his cameras with radar and ultraviolet. Hairline cracks had split the ice. Wisps of atmosphere bled from the open spaces beneath them, no more than a few molecules, but the air was white-hot compared to the vacuum on the surface.

The ice lifted and sagged. Many of the narrow gaps melted shut. Others widened.

"Christ," Koebsch said. "Oh Christ. Von, call him."

Her display went dark when Koebsch removed her from the group feed. He left open a single band to one of their overseers: the counter-electronic warfare AIs who swam in a tachyon-fast world of sabotage and control programs. The overseer would monitor her communications with Lam, sifting through each bit of data. It had the authority to edit or block his signals. It could also attack as it saw fit.

Lam had asked her to use 'Encryption I,' an obsolete code from weeks ago. The ESA was no longer using AZ codes at all. Crypto changed daily, sometimes hourly.

Was it a trick?

He shouldn't have the capacity to fox our systems, she thought, *not unless he's dedicated most of his computing power to assembling an SCP. Every time the real sunfish slept, he could have been arranging code... but he can't hate us that much, can he?*

The floor shuddered. "Hold on!" Ash yelled. Below her, Vonnie imagined the sunfish howling. They were a perfect diversion if Lam's utmost goal was revenge.

He'd arranged for her to contact him on his terms. If he'd prepared a cyber attack, it would start now.

"Lam?" she said.

8.

His tone was nothing like the aloof, calculated delivery of his prior broadcasts. He sounded human. He sounded rushed and afraid. —*Von, help me.*

"What do the sunfish want?"

—*I know you. You'll fight for me because I'm with the tribe. Because it's wrong. Because it's right. Your voice is why they listened to you.*

"Say again? You're not making sense."

—*Help me. I can't keep the tribe in harmony on my own. They'll divide again.*

"What do they want?"

—*You.*

Vonnie shook her head involuntarily and clenched her fists. She'd boasted to Dawson about meeting the sunfish, but the reality of climbing down into 07 was unthinkable. "Lam, I can't," she said.

—*You. You. You. You.*

She almost shut off communications. Instead, she glanced

through her limited display, grieving for him. Her overseer showed no indication of attack, but at best Lam seemed half-sane. He'd retained enough personality to imitate a man. The rest of him had eroded away in the dark.

That didn't mean he wasn't valuable. If they captured him, his mem files could provide an intimate look at the tribe's daily lives. Maybe she could guide his madness.

He's influencing the sunfish and on some level he's trying to reach me, too. "I want to help," she said. "Lam?"

—*They're listening.*

"Tell me what to do. Nobody wants to fight, but we don't understand our translations. The tribe is showing aggression and conquest. They're weakening the ice near our modules."

—*They're anxious. They're eager.*

"Why did they come here?"

—*You. You. You. You.*

She almost told her overseer to immobilize Lam with a slave-cast. If they regained control, O'Neal could use Lam's body to soothe the tribe or lead them back into the ice.

What if the sunfish perceived the change in Lam? Would they hurt him? They were so finely attuned to moods and motivations, reading each other's souls as easily as she read her datastreams...

'*Your voice is why they listened to you,*' he'd said.

She finally realized what that meant. "Damn it!" she said. Then she rammed her fist into her thigh, punishing herself for her stupidity. *I'm so tense, I stopped thinking like a sunfish. To them, what you say is far more than words. Your voice shows your state of mind.*

"Lam, are you relaying my broadcasts to the tribe in real time?"

she asked.

—*Relaying and translating.*

"We don't want to fight!" she yelled to the matriarchs. "We are allies! We hold a treaty with you!"

—*Yes. No. Yes. No.*

"I don't understand."

—*We are not Top Clan Eight-Six.*

"You're a new tribe. Of course. Bigger. Stronger. Four two, four two," she said, speaking faster and faster as she made sense of the phrase. *They doubled the number of individuals in their new clan*, she thought. *'Four two' might also compare the physical size of the larger breed to the smaller sunfish. There are so many nuances...* "We offer the same terms to you. Friendship. Power. Tools. Food."

She pictured Lam among them. He was broadcasting her words among the sunfish even as he called and danced, interpreting her meaning with his sonar and arm movements.

—*Food, yes*, he said. —*Allies, yes.*

"We can work together." Vonnie made it a statement, not a question.

—*The matriarchs need to discuss your offer and to determine their positions within the tribe*, he said. —*The hierarchy of this new clan is in flux.*

"Tell them we can provide more than food and tools. We offer knowledge. We offer peace."

No reply. Were they shrieking through the ice?

Muting her channel with Lam, Vonnie opened a separate link on her display. It was heavily secured, no vision, although she was convinced he'd never intended a cyber attack. "Koebsch, I don't feel their sonar. Did they stop screaming?"

"Yes," Koebsch said. "It's quieted down. Great work. Radar shows them physically conferencing with each other, and I listened to you on my display."

"Make sure Ribeiro knows what's happening."

"He shut down his gun platforms. I have everyone working on our translations or preparing more gifts as soon as it's safe to bring new mecha into the ice. The AIs are developing their translations, too. What did Lam mean about your voice?"

"Tom heard something right in me," she said with pride. "Every time we met, he was studying us. He was learning about people, then telling the matriarchs. The questions he asked weren't just to teach us their language or to get more food. He was testing me. Testing us."

Koebsch's voice was perplexed. "You're not representative of our entire race," he said.

"I am. Their perceptions run deeper than ours. Tom probably gleaned more about us than our scientists and AIs observed in him. He saw everything in me."

"That's scary."

"They don't hide anything from each other. Desire. Embar-rassment. Jealousy. They probably don't experience some of our emotions because nothing is secret to them. I wouldn't be surprised if they're aware of Dawson, not him specifically as a man but as a major entity in my life. They know about his greed and his disgust. They know he'll kill them if he can."

"Then why would they work with us?"

"They know I'll protect them. They know I'm ashamed of Dawson, and I have my own reasons to work with them. Because I like the attention. Because it makes me feel important." Her honesty was liberating, and she said more before she could stop herself. "Koebsch, I want to apologize for teasing you."

"I'm not sure what you mean."

"I've flirted with you. I let you think I was interested so you'd listen to me."

"I think you are interested," he said, startling her. Had he turned off the low-level AIs who recorded everything for analysis on Earth? If not, he might find himself reprimanded for encouraging her.

"Koebsch, we shouldn't—"

"I know it's tricky," he said. "I'm your boss and you like Ben, too. That doesn't mean I haven't thought about you, Von."

"Oh, uh," she stammered.

She hadn't been prepared for him to meet her apology with a confession. As an administrator, Peter Koebsch was adept at steering discussions to the subject of his choice.

She was glad he couldn't see her face when she blustered on. "I want to do better," she said. "That's what Tom saw in me, the right balance of intentions. That's why he pressed me about Ben. And you. When he asked those questions, you were in my feelings, too, Koebsch, my feelings for you and the knowledge that I could hurt you or help you if I was careful. That's what the sunfish need from us. They appreciate smart decisions and self-interest if it supports the tribe."

"We can talk about you and me later," Koebsch said, managing the topic of their conversation again. "How do we make the sunfish accept a new treaty?"

Relieved, she said, "It depends on the larger breed. We don't know enough about them. They must be intelligent. From the blood samples we scraped off my suit, they're also healthier than the smaller sunfish. Maybe they're not as desperate. What if the biosphere is more stable further down in the ice?"

"They came here when the smaller sunfish told them about us."

"Yes. That's promising. Let me call Lam. I also want to see our translations and talk to... O'Neal," she said.

She'd almost said *Ben*. She needed Koebsch to reconnect her display to the group feed, and he wasn't petty. He shouldn't balk if she used her lover's name, yet he was human, so she needed to tread lightly.

Koebsch said, "I can patch you to O'Neal and his feeds, but I can't give you full access, not while you're communicating with Lam."

"He's on our side."

"I can't take that risk."

"Okay, okay. Damn it. I want O'Neal and Ben and Ash," she said, hurrying over Ben's name in the middle. "I might need Henri, too."

"Four channels is too many. You can have O'Neal."

"I also need biology, geology, and ROM. Koebsch, we need to find out where the larger breed lives. Their environment will influence their vocabulary like the Top Clans are influenced by the upper sections of the ice. I also need Henri or Ash to rig a suit for me to walk through the cargo tube."

"Absolutely not."

"Nobody's going to wear it. I'll send the suit down by remote. We'll have to tweak a few things in its interior, but the sunfish will think it's me."

Koebsch might have shaken his head. A soft clatter filled their radio link. "It won't work," he said.

"It will. I know what I'm doing."

He grunted *hah* like an exasperated laugh. "It wouldn't be the first time," he said as if he was admitting to a bad habit. "Von, be careful."

"Yes, sir," she said. *I shouldn't have said 'sir,' she thought. I wanted to show respect, but he'll think I'm putting space between us now that I have what I want. Why can't I control my mouth?*

She glanced at her display as four windows lit up, then a fifth. Koebsch had authorized more feeds than she'd requested, linking her with three of her crewmates, himself, and an AI.

It was good to see them again. She didn't like being alone, and she drank in their postures and their faces, Koebsch with his handsome square face and blond hair even lighter than her own, Ben with his combative, sardonic gaze, Ash with her hard expression covered in girlish freckles, and O'Neal with his imperturbable calm.

Ben and Ash were working through radar sims. O'Neal had transcripts of the tribe's activity, which Ben had combined with his mock-ups.

In radar and infrared, the sunfish were a writhing mob. Twelve of them spilled over Submodule 07 like a wave, crawling among its struts and cables. The larger breed held most of the dominant positions near the underside of the group — most, but not all. Lam, and Charlotte were at the center of it. They debated with the larger sunfish.

LAM: Feel the metal / Breathe their scent.

LARGE MALES: *<indicating danger>* Beware!

SMALL SUNFISH: Great tools / Great strength.

CHARLOTTE: Their tribe is strong.

LARGE SUNFISH: We hear them / Sense them / Above the ice!

LARGE MALES: Death / Only death above.

CHARLOTTE: They rule the void / Great strength / They come and go like *<indicating massive predator>*.

LARGE FEMALE #1: They are the Old Ones!?

LAM: They are a new tribe / A strange tribe.

SMALL SUNFISH: Strange life above the ice!

CHARLOTTE: They rule the void / We can rule the ice together / Their tools / Our warriors.

Brigit struggled to join Charlotte and Lam near the bottom of the pack. She rasped her arms against the larger females, then snapped her beak, challenging them.

BRIGIT: We fight / We win.

LARGE FEMALES: No / We hold the balance / Mid Clan Top Clan / We hold more weight.

SMALL MALES: We fight!

LAM: Ghost Clan changes weight / Changes balance.

CHARLOTTE AND BRIGIT: We are hardier than you / We fight / Mid Clan joins Top Clan joins Ghost Clan.

"How old is this transcript?" Vonnie asked.

"It's happening now," O'Neal said. "They've been repeating the same arguments without a lot of change for several minutes. Only the name 'Ghost Clan' is new."

"'Ghost Clan' is what they call us?"

"Yeah. Our name was a key factor in how their conversation has evolved. I think the larger breed were skeptical. Even if sunfish can't lie, they didn't believe what they'd been told about us until they saw our mecha. They kept referring to us a 'Top Top Clan,' which is probably an insult."

Vonnie nodded. The sterile, upper reaches of the frozen sky were populated by the smaller breed because they were outcasts and refugees, the losers of an ancient war. They'd survived endless tragedies — and she laughed with excitement. "If the larger breed calls itself 'Mid Clan, not 'Bottom' or 'Low Clan,' they must be aware of *more* sunfish further down."

"More sunfish or something else," O'Neal said. His words were circumspect, but the skin at the corners of his eyes crinkled in pleasure and friendship. "Don't get carried away, Von. The larger breed uses their own dialect. It's altered how the smaller sunfish speak to them, and we're missing some connotations."

Vonnie didn't care. "Ash, I need a scout suit."

"You can't be that stupid," Ash said.

"Hear me out. Nobody's going down there. I just need a suit to act like me."

Ben wore an approving grin. "Sneaky."

"Wait," Koebsch said. "A suit won't have the right sound or weight without someone inside it. The sunfish will know something's wrong."

"We'll pack it with transplants from the med lab. The clone stock smells human and has the right mass," Vonnie explained as Ash said, "Oh, gross."

Koebsch shook his head. "Those transplants are expensive, and it wouldn't work. Dead meat won't generate a bioelectric field. Dawson proved the sunfish were able to sense you inside your suit at close range."

"We'll rig a few gadgets to produce a weak electrical field and sounds like breathing and a heartbeat."

"Then we could pack the suit with anything that matches your weight. They can't smell what's inside."

"The suit won't have the right density unless we use muscle and bone. Their sonar—"

Koebsch interrupted her. "Are you talking about stitching together a corpse from spare parts? The mess would be... You're asking too much. That would waste most of our clone stock. What if there's an emergency?"

What if we used Rauno or Beth? she thought.

The bodies of Rauno Pärnits and Beth Collinsworth were also stored in the med lab. There was nowhere to bury them on Europa. Nor was there an easy way to send them home.

Both of her friends probably would have liked the idea of participating even in death. Every crewmember had signed a donor release, a standard provision for deep space missions — but while Vonnie envision pulling Beth from the freezer, she couldn't suggest it. Ash would yell at her. So would Koebsch. She wondered if she'd spent too much time with the tribes. The sunfish were squeamish about nothing and had no taboos.

"Fine," she said. "Ben, Ash, let's rig something without transplants. Call Henri. He can assist. I want to get a human presence into the ice."

"Roger that," Ben said. He was standing back-to-back with her in Module 06, and, immersed in their displays, he bent around and scratched her hip.

Vonnie smiled.

"I'm not convinced," Koebsch said. "You never met Tom in a suit. What if they ask you to climb out of it?"

Ben argued for her. "She has a good plan."

"This is between Von and I," Koebsch said. His expression was neutral, but Vonnie heard the flint in his tone.

Koebsch had noticed Ben's intimate touch on her hip. All of them knew the gesture had been possessive. Ben had deliberately taunted the other man. It made her a little mad at him. It made her mad at herself.

Our social groups are so convoluted, she thought. *That's why we almost nuked the sunfish. We expect everything to be a trick. They merely act. Their tribes are always changing, but they repeat the same arrangements over and over with the matriarchs and the intelligent males leading the rest. We have more variations because we're separate from each other. We hint and lie and hold ourselves back.*

She wanted more sincerity in her life, so she was brisk, chastising both men for wasting time. "If the sunfish realize I'm not in the suit, we'll admit it. They use expendable males as scouts. That's how we'll explain things if they ask. We'll say we can afford to lose our suits but not our people."

"All right," Koebsch said.

Ben lifted his hand as if to touch her again, yet reconsidered.

Vonnie turned away from him, hoping neither man was upset. She loved Ben, and she was fond of Koebsch, and she marveled again that three people could develop so many different relation-ships — colleague, competitor, lover, boss. "O'Neal, have the matriarchs determined their hierarchy?"

"I think they're waiting for us," O'Neal said. "Lam is telling stories. So is Tom. They're describing you. How we approach the new tribe may affect how they choose their leaders. Right now

Charlotte and Lam seem to have reached a détente with the larger females."

"Ben, if you warm up a spare suit in the armory, I'll install the gear," Ash said. "Henri's online. He can run the nanoforge. Von, we need ten minutes."

"Make it five."

"Roger that," Ben said. He opened a ROM program inside Module 01, prepping a suit as Ash left her station.

Vonnie glanced through O'Neal's transcripts, where his AI had weeded out the most redundant threads. Among the sunfish, information was repeated until every member of the tribe confirmed. They touched and sang in a perpetual loop, reacting to each other as much as they did to other stimuli.

Unfortunately, there was a significant level of meaningless noise in their group mind. Too many of them were animals.

Short-period isotopes contaminated the frozen sky. Lethal veins of sulfuric acid and salt also stained the ice. Even when the Top Clans had enough to eat, their food chain was laced with toxins, and they rarely had unrelated breeding pairs.

The smaller sunfish were nearly clones of each other. They lacked genetic diversity, and it had robbed them of sentience, especially among their males. Dawson estimated the intelligence of many of them was equal to that of wolves.

The savages were a drag on the tribe. They resisted plans that required forethought. When they could be manipulated, they were an asset to the matriarchs, who used them as raiders and front line soldiers, but the sad irony was that other Top Clans were also populated with savages. The sunfish appeared to need berserkers in order to survive their neighbors' berserkers, a self-perpetuating cycle in which they attacked and were attacked. Yes, the savages used stealth and elaborate formations in combat, but spatial relations were innate to their species. After centuries of war, intelligence had taken a back seat to brutality.

The ESA had observed the matriarchs endeavoring to improve their offspring. They told which pairs to mate. They committed infanticide on children who exhibited obvious birth defects, although hereditary and immunological diseases were less detectable and therefore common. The matriarchs tried to stay ahead of the issue by culling their eggs, but they were undermined by the savages, who bred at will and culled the wrong eggs. The savages preferred eggs with multiple embryos, which often hatched as more savages, and the matriarchs allowed it.

Was that to avoid fighting each other or because the matriarchs wanted more savages?

It's a double-edged sword, Vonnie thought. *The intelligent sunfish can't expand their colonies because they spend too much time controlling the disruptive elements inside their own homes. On the other hand, dealing with the savages has increased the matriarchs' abilities to scheme and coax and think ahead.*

We don't know if the larger sunfish have savages in their tribes. We don't even know if they have matriarchs, although their females seem to be in charge.

Did the smaller matriarchs goad the larger sunfish into following their lead with the threat of violence?

Vonnie believed that was exactly what had happened. Studying her transcripts, she saw an uneven boil of anticipation mixed with paranoia. The larger breed exhibited anger. The smaller matriarchs were slyly triumphant.

"Who do we approach first?" she asked. "The larger sunfish look like they've deferred to the smaller ones."

"Not quite," O'Neal said. "The dynamic is subtle. The larger sunfish have had a relaxing effect on the group. They've influenced the overall mood."

Vonnie saw what he meant when she compared his sims to their AI scores. The larger breed moved among the smaller sunfish like sea lions among seals. They were louder and bulkier. Physically and mentally, they slowed the activity within the squirming tribe. "Are they smarter?" she asked.

"Unknown. There's definitely a higher level of semantic content among the larger breed. They use more signifiers, more complex phrases and vocabulary."

"Then I should approach them."

"I think that would be a mistake. Look at this." O'Neal opened a new sim, a data summary gleaned from the females' debates. "The larger breed came here because the smaller sunfish showed them metal tools and Lam, and because the smaller sunfish demonstrated unusual conviction in demanding a treaty with them. They weren't submissive. They told the larger breed to join them or lose the opportunity to join us."

"You're saying the smaller matriarchs took the initiative and they want to keep it."

"That's how they've maintained control over their savages. They need to remain in dominant positions or the lesser males will rebel. This new tribe is precarious. It's volatile."

"I need your official recommendation," Koebsch said. "Are you advising us to stay out of the ice?"

"If we don't go in, the sunfish will leave," O'Neal said.

Vonnie grimaced. Why was Koebsch second-guessing his decision now? *He must have heard from Berlin*, she thought, glancing at her clocks. Enough time had elapsed for a response from Earth, although given the radio lag, their agency and government leaders were woefully behind unfolding events.

At the moment, the datastreams reaching Earth would show Top Clan Eight-Six plunging into the ice and Dawson yelling that the sunfish planned to open a geyser.

Too many people were pulling Koebsch in too many directions. Berlin could demand that he follow protocols. The proxies could hound him. Later, Earth's governments and the media would criticize any decision he made — and none of that mattered. The weight of history belonged to Koebsch.

Characteristically, he said, "I don't like it. This is happening too fast. We're not prepared."

"The sunfish don't prepare," Vonnie said.

"They'll never arrange a meeting at a conference table," O'Neal agreed. "They don't mark time like we do. Most of their actions are spontaneous."

Ash had been watching her clocks, too. "Sir, you heard from Berlin?" she asked.

"My orders are to exercise extreme caution," Koebsch said.

He was obviously dissatisfied with this instruction, and Ben laughed. "'Extreme caution.' That's pointless advice. They're covering their asses."

"Ben, shut up," Vonnie said more harshly than she'd intended. "Koebsch, stop worrying about Earth. They're too far behind the curve. We're the ones on the front line. We can do something great here today."

"She's right," O'Neal said. "This opportunity is unprecedented. It may have been hundreds of years since the two breeds worked together."

"That's why I don't like it. We can't predict their next move," Koebsch said.

"We know enough to barter with them," O'Neal said. "The Top Clan wants more status and a better home. The Mid Clan wants our power."

"They might have other agendas," Koebsch said. "Can they have children with each other? The smaller matriarchs may want to improve the health and size of their offspring. The larger breed could want savages for their own wars. If we accept a treaty with them... What kind of deal are we making?"

Vonnie blinked. She regarded Koebsch as a good man, but she also thought of him as a desk jockey, not an astronaut, much less a scientist. *I should give him more credit*, she thought even as she haggled with him. "We can't answer those questions if we don't go down there," she said. "The sunfish won't accept a treaty without touching one of us."

"Koebsch, we need to do this," O'Neal said.

"Two of the smaller males are banging on 07 again," Ben said. "It's not a concerted effort, but they're also screeching at the ice."

"They're restless," O'Neal said. "The larger sunfish are impatient, and their attitude is transferring to the rest. They won't keep waiting. They'll scavenge what they can from the mecha and leave. They may attack each other."

"Don't miss our chance," Vonnie said.

Koebsch waved his hands as if forming a barricade to protect himself from Vonnie and O'Neal. "Enough," he said. "I'm convinced, but I need you to realize we're playing with fire. Who are their enemies? What are the Low Clans if they exist? Will the other Top Clans unite against us after we form an alliance with the larger breed?"

"We can always back out," Vonnie said. "We're literally above their wars. We don't need to get involved. We can be teachers and diplomats, not generals."

"Von, they may not let us stand on the sidelines," Koebsch said. His gray-blue eyes were clouded with warning. He looked like he was about to order her to stand down. Then he gestured for her to proceed. "Bring your suit into the air lock," he said. "We're going in."

9.

"Activate all combat systems," Vonnie told Ash. It was a day for blindsiding each other. Koebsch had surprised Vonnie with his comprehensive grasp of the tribe's prospects. Now she surprised Ash, who'd never imagined she would want weapons.

"You didn't... Why?" Ash asked.

"Some of the smaller sunfish fought Ribeiro's mecha," Vonnie said. "Both breeds might have been among the groups who fought me. They understand guns, and they know when our sensors are hot. Turn everything on. Radar. Spotlight. Welding tool. Can you mag-lock an excavation charge on the wrist?"

"What good would that do?"

"We don't need to detonate the charge. We want to intimidate them."

"Roger that." Ash busied herself with the armory controls inside Module 01. "The suit is walking toward my air lock. When it's outside, I'll accelerate to a run. Your time of arrival is five minutes."

"I'm not sure we have that long," Ben said. "The smaller males are agitated. They're screaming at the matriarchs."

"I see them," Vonnie said.

Four of the smaller males were chopping at Submodule 07 with hunks of alumalloy from the destroyed mecha. They dug at the seams of the secondary hatch. Was it laced with Tom's scent from the many times he'd entered and exited?

Shrieking, posturing, the matriarchs demanded that they stop: —*Drop your tools! Obey us!*

Two larger males tried to grab the smaller males. A smaller male cut one of his opponent's arms. The wound was shallow, but the blood excited all of the sunfish. The smaller males spun as if to attack the matriarchs, widening their beaks.

"Lam, I'm coming in," Vonnie said.

—*We hear you. I hear you.*

She hoped he was still relaying her broadcasts to the tribe. She deliberately insulted them. "Control your males!" she yelled. "Control them or I'll control them for you. My tribe values self-discipline and cooperation. Only lesser animals cannot govern themselves."

—Yes. No. Yes.

Was he cautioning her not to offend the matriarchs? She felt like she was on a thin line as she said, "Are you animals or are you Clans? Poor leadership is why you're scattered and weak. My tribe wants to build a new empire, but we need healthy allies, not savages. We need Clans."

—No. Yes. They're listening. Yes.

The separate groups of sunfish whirled abruptly. The larger breed and the matriarchs leapt into the air and combined against Submodule 07, pinning the savages on its metal surface.

The savages bit and thrashed, but the fighting stopped when the matriarchs allowed them to grope at the larger male's injury. Terrestrial predators would have been further aroused by the gore. The sunfish were soothed by the taste of blood. They shared a new song of bonding as Lam said:

—You're entering the ice?

"Yes. Soon." Vonnie muted her radio link with him and glanced at O'Neal. "What do we call ourselves, Ghost Clan what?" she asked.

"I haven't parsed their identifiers," O'Neal said. "The way they count is more than fours and eights. I think their tribe names also refer to the ratio of females to males, breeding pairs and able hunters."

"Which is better, big numbers or small?"

"Big numbers denote larger tribes and more desirable homes. Top Clan Eight-Six had a different name before the survivors of Two-Four joined them. The larger breed, the Mid Clan, has used several numbers since they appeared. They're experimenting. I don't think they'll determine their new name until we resolve things with them."

"What's the biggest number you've heard?" Koebsch asked.

"The Mid Clan called themselves Twelve-Eight in our first recordings of this group," O'Neal said.

"Let's use our own math," Koebsch said. "They know we're different. Von, the proxies want you to call us Ghost Clan Forty-Fifty."

"The tribes don't use tens or any quantity above sixteen," O'Neal said. "Fifty isn't a sunfish number. Even forty is too much."

"That's why we should use human numbers," Koebsch said. "We're bigger than they are. We're stronger."

"Size is less important to them than exquisitely described proportions," O'Neal said. "War parties always round to the weakest amount. A thirteen-member pack is a twelve. A seven-armed sunfish is called a six. They never describe a tunnel or a cave as a single place. Everything is connected, including their concepts of tomorrow and yesterday. To them, Vonnie and Tom were a pair. When they separated, Tom became a zero until he returned to the tribe. Who knows how they thought of Vonnie after she was on her own. As far as they're concerned, twos are indivisible. Time isn't linear. Directions go both ways. We keep misinterpreting their actions because we think up is down and we see them as individuals when they only hear and smell the group."

"Roger that," Koebsch said slowly.

One of the most profound hurdles in dealing with the sunfish was that the tribes and humankind had opposite perspectives of which species stood above the other. To the sunfish, Europa's ocean was the center of their universe.

It was an insular view. It was a natural response to their sensory limitations.

On Earth, even the most primitive sea organisms had been aware of the sun. The open surface, the light, the changing weather and the shorelines had eventually allowed for plant life, then amphibians, then reptiles and birds and mammals. Men had watched the stars, inventing myths to explain those distant suns, then developing calendars, navigational charts, and finally hurling themselves into space.

Europa's center drew the sunfish to safety. They did not try to escape their world as humankind had always yearned to fly. They followed Europa's depths as far as they were able, climbing "up" through the ice like a man would climb a ladder.

Even their terms for "Top," "Mid" and "Low" had been misconstrued by humankind. "Top Clan" was not a claim of supremacy. The name was derogatory. To them, the surface was the bottom of everything.

No one from Earth could say if Europa's ocean was a safe, warm core. ESA models suggested the water was a vortex of riptides and scalding thermal vents. It also held stifling levels of sulfuric acid. The prime regions for life probably existed among the mountains and seas suspended in the middle sections of the frozen sky, presumably where the Low Clans resided. The Top and Mid Clans might want to climb only so far "up," stopping short of the ocean — but to do so, they would need to invade the Low Clans, either an invasion by force or an invasion of ideas.

We can teach them, although we need a firm hand, Vonnie thought. *They won't respect a gentle touch.*

She was uncomfortable with assuming the role of the tough guy, but stature was integral to their culture. She could no more present herself as their equal than she could speak English without pronouns or verbs. At best, she would sound muddled. She couldn't make them listen unless she struck a brazen tone.

Equally important was how the empty scout suit acted.

"Ash, stomp your feet," Vonnie said. "I want you to make as much noise you can."

"Roger that." On their group feed, Ash danced her arms and legs inside a ROM program. She had been running the suit from 01 to 06. Now she exaggerated her stride, and her hazel eyes glinted. Maybe she enjoyed masquerading as a heavy-footed monster. She had been frightened by the sunfish too many times not to relish banging on the ice as Lam called:

—We hear you. We're waiting.

"I'm approaching the air lock," Vonnie told him. "You'll hear more vibrations when I open the top hatch, then equalize the tube. Stay back from the bottom hatch."

—We're waiting. We're singing.

"The matriarchs are calling again," O'Neal reported. "They're advising the group beneath the FNEE modules. Eight of those sunfish have left. They're moving down and westward through the ice."

"Where are they going? Toward me?" Vonnie asked.

"Yes. They'll reach the cavern with Submodule 07 before your suit clears the tube."

"Are they smaller males or matriarchs?" Koebsch asked.

"Smaller males," O'Neal said.

"Christ," Ben muttered as Vonnie internalized a sharp curse of her own. *Eight males will alter the nature of the pack*, she thought. *They'll be more violent, less communicative. They're sending warriors.*

Why would they do that?

The suit was fifty seconds from reaching Module 06. "Can I see the proxies' sims?" she asked.

"I'm sorry," Koebsch said. "Your station is on quarantine until we're certain about Lam, but the proxies are convincing. Their decision was 'Ghost Clan Forty-Fifty.'"

"Their decision was by vote, and it included every ranking bureaucrat in the bunch," O'Neal said. "They don't know what they're talking about. Bigger isn't necessarily better to the sunfish, and the more valued number comes first. That's how we knew Top Clan Eight-Six was more successful than Two-Four, not because their numbers were larger, because of the arrangement. 'Forty-Fifty' is a backwards name. Believe me. Ghost Clan Twenty-Sixteen is better."

"Koebsch, who do you trust, O'Neal or the proxies?" Vonnie asked.

"We're under orders," he said.

"I know, I know! Stop reminding us. Earth wants to tell you what to do after we've done it. You're going to have to go with your gut."

"Von, the suit is outside your module," Ash said. "I put ten lab tabs in the chest pack."

"Roger that."

Vonnie touched her display. Because she wore a pressure suit, she was well-prepared to act as if she was inside the scout suit. To begin, she cloned the ROM program from Ash's station. Virtual immersion and tactile cues completed the illusion. Her station projected a holographic field inside her visor. Then her gloves and boots squeezed slightly. So did the headband inside her helmet. Microscopic relays created physical feedback, which her station factored into the simulation.

Vonnie shut her eyes at the stabbing pinch of a migraine. Her station adjusted its holography. The headache went away.

She appeared to be wearing the scout suit. It stood five meters from Module 06 and the opaque tent that housed the cargo lock. The exterior of 06 blazed with spotlights and cameras. On her visor, she saw infrared beams and fine laser grids distributed among the lights.

She advanced on the tent clumsily. Using a virtual program was a learned art. She couldn't actually walk because her body was inside the confines of 06. She'd crash into the wall or Ben or Dawson. *Sorry I stepped on your wrinkled old face, Billy*, she thought, needing a joke. She needed to relax.

Every nerve impulse was magnified and augmented by the ROM program. Tipping one heel caused the scout suit to step forward. Lifting and aiming her feet could set its boots on ladder rungs. Only its gloves operated with fine motor control, mimicking her hands exactly.

She unsealed the tent's outer flap, which led to an entry bubble lined with vents. "Stage one, go," she said. Her visor darkened as UV lights baked the scout suit, cooking off any Earth smells and microbes. Next she was blasted with melted ice peppered with native dust.

Alarm bars filled her display. Vonnie jerked her arm in front of her face, an astronaut's instinct to guard her helmet. She thought the decontamination gear had malfunctioned. Then she realized their defense net was alerting everyone. The sunfish had screeched at the familiar drone of the machinery. Some of them were banging on Submodule 07 again.

Vibrations shook the tent before Vonnie felt a jarring *thud* in the ice. "O'Neal, what happened!?" she yelled.

Ben answered first. "The new pack of smaller males are closing fast. Radar shows a half-ton collapse in their tunnel. They tore down its roof behind them like they're containing a threat — like they're containing *you*."

"The matriarchs are losing control, although Tom is advocating for us," O'Neal said.

He posted new transcripts on Vonnie's display. The sunfish had responded to the cave-in with their shrill cries, warning her, welcoming her, a flood of clashing intent. Tom was exultant. So were many of the larger breed. Lam moved among them with body shapes requesting patience, but the smaller males convulsed in their hysteria.

TOM: Ghost Clan is coming!

SMALLER MALES: Intruders / Strange life!

CHARLOTTE AND BRIGIT: We hear them / Great size / Great strength approaches us!

LARGER FEMALES: *<indicating curiosity>* Ghost Clan is Metal Clan?

SMALLER MALES: Strange life / Danger!

CHARLOTTE AND BRIGIT: *<urging composure>* Ghost Clan *is* dangerous / Not dangerous / Great size / Yes / Treaty / Yes / Ghost Clan is metal and flesh.

TOM: Strange flesh / Strange bodies / Strong and smart.

SMALLER MALES: Attack! Attack!

"If you're really going down there, get ready for a fight,"

O'Neal said. "You may need to immobilize several of them before they'll quit."

Vonnie winced at the memory of stomping on two sunfish. She had sobbed in the wet carnage when they burst.

I don't want to hurt you, she thought.

"If my transcripts are correct, the larger breed hopes you'll come in swinging," O'Neal said. "They need you to pacify the smaller males."

"Lam?" she asked. "Lam, tell the matriarchs! If I fight the smaller males... Will anyone else attack me?"

She knew them too well. Their hair-trigger reflex to kill or be killed was as unstoppable as the innate human need to protect the eyes and face.

"Lam!?" she yelled.

His voice was steady, but he merely echoed the conflicting moods of the tribe. —*Yes. No. Yes. Yes.*

"He's useless. We can't rely on him," Koebsch said.

"Let me grab him with a slavecast," Ash suggested. "We'll take over. We need him to protect Von."

"We need him to talk to them," Vonnie said. "If you lock him down, they'll reject him. He won't move like a sunfish anymore. He'll move like a probe."

"He *is* a probe."

"He's something else now. He's one of them. Koebsch, don't try to fix him. We could lose whatever qualities make him like a sunfish."

"Ash, I want you on standby," Koebsch said. "If he makes one wrong move..."

"Yes, sir."

Fans had cooled Vonnie's suit to -142° Celsius, the hellish temperature in the cavern. Shaking, she forced herself to exhibit the same composure as the matriarchs.

She opened her chest pack. It held ten "lab tabs," the samples drawn weekly from her skin, blood, stools and urine. Twice a month, the ESA crew also gave bone marrow. Living on the surface, they were bathed in an unimaginable sleet of radiation. Their modules and suits couldn't protect them entirely, and, working with the medical teams on Earth, Harmeet devised individually-tailored regimens of genesmithing and nanotech. Someday they would need surgeries to root out various cancers. For now, each crewmember produced an extensive library of fluids and tissues. Ash had stocked the chest pack with Vonnie's most recent samples.

The tabs were too tiny for her gloves. Like any mecha, however, the scout suit had auto programs. It could efficiently stack supply crates or perform construction welds by itself.

Vonnie opened a checklist with an up-and-down movement of her eyes. Then she directed her right hand to remove one tab with the magnetic pad on her ring finger. Another magnetic pad activated on her thumb. The tab unlocked. She blotted its contents on the suit's collar and wrists where a woman might dab perfume on herself before a date.

She snorted at the idea. Most of the urine boiled off in the cold, but the sunfish would detect every stray molecule like a man would respond to a tempting fragrance.

I wish I had the guts to climb down in person, she thought. *Will we ever go back into the ice?*

"Sir, what's your decision about our tribe name?" she asked

Koebsch. She knew he didn't want to hear such formality from her, but the record of their next few minutes would be meticulously analyzed on Earth. Despite what anyone believed, she wanted to defer to him. She owed him that much. She knew she wasn't easy to work with, no more than the sunfish were an easy puzzle to solve.

"We'll go with O'Neal's analysis," Koebsch said. "Tell them we're Ghost Clan Twenty-Sixteen."

"Roger that," she said, clamping down on a victorious laugh. Her adrenaline was too powerful. If she laughed, it would be a titter, and she didn't want sound like a frightened ape in their recordings. Everything she did now would be studied by millions of people for years to come. She didn't want to overlook a single detail.

She walked from decon into the central part of the tent. The floor was steel plating. The hatch was mechanized. It would open with a voice command.

"Stage two, go," she said.

As the hatch raised, the tube shook with a grinding cacophony as the savages drummed and scraped on the bottom end. *Bam bam bam bam. Eeeeeeeee. Bam bam.*

Anarchy had reclaimed the tribe. Ben's radar showed the savage males tussling with Lam and the larger breed, who were thrown aside by the smaller males' ferocity. The matriarchs had retreated. Did they believe the smaller males would tire out?

Her spotlight swept downward and her visor modified her radar signals into holo imagery. The ladder was starkly illuminated. Nevertheless, her claustrophobia returned as she climbed in, so she called Ash, diverting her fear with shop talk. "What did you put inside the suit?"

"Con foam and plastic," Ash said. "Henri fabricated an assembly that looks like a rib cage and a skull. The plastic almost has the same density as bone, and we made hollows and thick spots in the foam like organs and muscle. We also put a relay inside. It's on sleep mode and producing a weak electrical field, not quite the same as a person. That's the best we could do on short notice."

"Fantastic. Thank you." On the ladder, Vonnie lifted her gaze for last look overhead. All she could see was the ceiling of the tent. "Seal me in."

"I'm doing it now."

The hatch closed with a *boom*, eliciting more screams and banging from the savage males.

Caught in the tube, Vonnie felt her mind divide. The vulnerable part of her went away. The proficient, economical woman took over. "I want a link to our translation AIs," she said. "Equalize the tube with the cavern. Lower the oxygen mix. Let's bring more food and tools into the tent above me. The mecha should make as much noise as possible."

"Roger that," Ash said. "Pumps on."

"Here's your link," O'Neal said, posting new AI menus on her visor.

The tube hummed as life support kicked in, reducing the air pressure and screening out the O2. Sunfish metabolism was too receptive. If the air surrounding her was oxygen-rich when she emerged, they would convert it to energy. The savages would grow wilder.

Vonnie stepped off the ladder. Despite her adrenaline, a final thought nagged at her. *The Top Clans' written and oral histories tell stories about lost colonies and foreign races, but their concepts are rarely abstract.*

"O'Neal, are you sure our name is correct?" she asked. "It's weird that they even have a word for 'ghost.'"

"Their shapes for it mean 'unseen' or 'immaterial,'" he said. "You have to remember, over time they've found traces of other beings without physically encountering them. Bones. Spoor. Prints. Those creatures are phantoms to them. That's what we are, too. Tom has met you. The larger sunfish believe his accounts, and they've touched our mecha and Submodule 07, but I'm not sure they know what to think."

No more doubt, she decided. *Not for me, not for them. If the two breeds haven't worked together for centuries, this meeting is more than a stepping stone. It could be the foundation of something much greater.*

I need to confront the tribe like a legend. Shock and awe. I need to impress them.

Her helmet was equipped with a voice box for communicating with workers who weren't in suits. She upped her volume to deafening levels, using sonar as well as frequencies in the human range. She took one breath to center herself. Then she activated her speakers and screeched:

—WE ARE GHOST CLAN TWENTY-SIXTEEN! WE ARE BREACHING THE ICE! MOVE BACK! WE ARE GHOST CLAN TWENTY-SIXTEEN!

10.

The tube reverberated with the sound. It amplified and distorted her screams into a roar. Then she punched the hatch. She dropped through.

Landing beside Submodule 07, Vonnie bent down onto her left hand and her toes. The pose was a hulking, predatory crouch. She held her right arm across her chest, ready to shield herself, ready to fight.

—*WE ARE TWENTY-SIXTEEN!* she screeched.

The smaller males recoiled, knuckling their arms against their bodies to protect their ears. As her spotlight swept the cavern, they flinched like they'd been burned.

One clacked his beak, snapping and howling. —*Attack!*

Lam spoke for the matriarchs and the larger breed as they coalesced into a defiant, more unified pack. They shrieked at her, but they also called among themselves, lashing their pedicellaria. —*We are here! We are here!*

Vonnie understood some of their actions. Their hierarchy was still being decided. The process was unfolding quickly now. They contracted and squirmed, testing each individual in the group, trying new combinations, although Vonnie saw more questions than certainty in their body shapes.

Charlotte emerged as one of the strongest-willed matriarchs. She drew the other females into alignment with her by encouraging the hostility of the savage males. She riled the males with her arms, jabbing, squeezing, forcing the other females to support her or allow the savages to dominate. Then she screamed her own challenges at Vonnie:

—*You are wrong! You are strange!*

Vonnie's hopes sank, but she kept her shoulders up and her fist cocked. —*I am your friend*, she cried. —*Your scouts have met with me for many days.*

Charlotte denied it. —*You have her scent, but your metal holds something wrong and dead. You are not you. You are crippled. You are weak.*

"She knows the suit isn't Von," Koebsch muttered as Ash said, "The males are going to attack."

—*WE ARE GHOST CLAN TWENTY-SIXTEEN!* Vonnie roared at them. —*Don't make me crush you! We have always sent our machines into the ice. You know our suits can kill and build and hear in ways beyond any sunfish.*

In fact, she realized, the tribe's discovery of her ruse might convey more status to her. Sending the empty suit in her place should make her appear more like a matriarch while the suit served as a lesser male.

Charlotte trembled. Then she made her choice. Lam seemed to anticipate it. He and Charlotte leapt into the air, but they did not attack. They corralled the savage males. Lam shoved two of them away from Vonnie before Charlotte grabbed two more, keeping the males from a confrontation with her.

—*Your kind is strange*, Charlotte called.

—*I _am_ a friend!* Vonnie cried. She could never match their frantic wriggling, yet she lifted her left hand and gave partial control of it to the AI programs, which made her fingers jerk in an approximation of sunfish shapes. —*I control this suit, but my tribemates are not different from yours. We live. We breathe. We mate. We die.*

The savage males shrieked. Lam and Tom held onto them. At the same time, Brigit was addressing the other sunfish. Charlotte joined her song.

The females of both breeds grasped at each other. Their group tightened. They called to Vonnie, an avalanche of meaning too fast for Lam to wholly translate. *—We are bigger smaller stronger different smarter same.*

—Yes, Vonnie cried. She didn't know if they'd agreed that sunfish and human beings weren't completely unlike or if they'd merely stated the similarities between their cousin breeds. She was glad to find anything positive to say... but her immediate "yes" might have been a mistake.

The matriarchs howled again. *—We would be Thirty!* they screamed.

"O'Neal, what are they telling me?" Vonnie asked. Studying her display, she hedged her response. She cried at the matriarchs. *—Your ambition is useful. Your diseases can be cured. Together we will rule the ice.*

"Don't back off," O'Neal said. "I think they want our treaty and they're going to accept it, but my guess is they usually argue with each other for days. Their pecking order is so intricate. They want to haggle with you."

"I can't do this forever," Vonnie said. She had been in her session with Tom for an hour before he'd abandoned her. Then she'd endured another busy hour as Top Clan Eight-Six returned with the larger breed. Excitement would only carry her so far. Stress was taking its toll. Could the sunfish read her growing fatigue in how she wore the suit?

Of course they can, she thought, shaking off her exhaustion. She scraped her left glove over the ice like a skater in a turn, marking the cavern floor, claiming it.

—*We will rule this world*, she said. —*We can take it without you, but we want allies and guides.*

—*Attack!* screamed two of the smaller males.

Vonnie didn't look at them. —*Decide*, she said.

—*Danger! Attack!* the males screamed, exhorting the others to swarm her.

—*Decide before we crush your savages*, she said. —*They cannot wait. You cannot wait. Decide before we kill them and war exists between us again.*

The larger females called insistently to Vonnie and to the smaller matriarchs. —*Who leads? Who leads?*

—*I lead*, she said, pointing at herself, not her friends overhead. She wondered if she should have used a plural noun by saying '*We lead.*' The sunfish never did anything in solitude except for ragged, expendable scouts like Tom. Even scouts typically moved in fours.

If her crewmates had activated more suits to present an even-numbered group, she might have said '*we*,' but the tribes were influenced by standouts like Charlotte and Brigit and Lam. They had chiefs and lieutenants. More important, she remembered how Lam had convinced her to enter the cavern.

You'll fight for me because I'm with the tribe, he'd said. *Because it's wrong. Because it's right. Your voice is why they listened to you.*

Teaching individuality to the sunfish was a crucial aspect of teaching them to work with humankind. She also wanted to make herself essential to their future. If anyone on Earth complained, she would ask why nobody else had been in the ice. She was the one who'd endured failures and pain. She wanted to personally offer herself to the tribe, so she squared her shoulders and moved closer, reiterating her decree.

—*I lead*, she said.

They reached a verdict. It rippled among them like an electric current, altering their group.

Vonnie glimpsed fragments of meaning in their body shapes, but it was O'Neal who latched onto an explanation. "The larger breed has accepted the smaller sunfish," he said. "They're sharing their status with the matriarchs and the intelligent males like Tom and Lam."

In front of her, the mixed sunfish contracted into a knot. Just as suddenly, they expanded, thrashing wildly as the matriarchs rejoiced.

—*We are Mid Clan Six-Six!* they cried.

The emotion was too much for the smaller males. The eight of them scurried and twitched, slashing at each other. —*Attack!* they screamed.

—*No*, Vonnie said. —*Mid Clan joins Ghost Clan. Treaty. Same tribe. There is no danger here.*

—*Strange life! Attack!*

"Damn it," O'Neal said calmly as the smaller males snapped at her. Then they separated themselves into two fateful lines of four. "Von, here they come."

Vonnie tried to stop them. She bunched her arms and legs like a sunfish taking the offensive. She knew her size wouldn't scare them, but they'd backed down earlier when she combined the appropriate body language with her voice.

—*WE ARE TWENTY-SIXTEEN!* she roared.

The eight males jumped in crisscrossing waves of four. The front wave bounced off the cavern floor. The trailing wave went into the ceiling. In the air, many of them shoved each other to complicate their trajectories.

Closing on her from multiple directions, they somersaulted. They led with their gaping beaks.

Vonnie batted three of them aside with her first blow. She smacked her metal fist up through their bodies, ricocheting her glove from one male to the next like a dot-to-dot holo game.

The fourth male flew past her head as the fifth snatched at her thigh, but she rocked sideways to meet the fourth one, catching him between her shoulder and her helmet, jamming his beak against her cheekbone.

She felt the arms of a sixth male graze her back. Then she slammed her knee into the side of Submodule 07, bruising the male on her thigh. Stunned, he loosened. She pounded him with her fist and he peeled away.

She swung to face the rest.

In front of her, the larger sunfish and the matriarchs called among themselves. A few had retreated. Others lashed and snapped, unable to resist their blood thirst.

Three of the smaller males rebounded from the cavern walls, taking new angles above and behind Vonnie. Her radar targeting was faster. She batted the nearest male with another non-lethal blow, striking the hard cartilage-and-muscle of his arms rather than slamming her fist into his underside.

Did they understand mercy? The matriarchs were also rough

with the savages, and Vonnie screamed: —*Control yourselves! Control your males!*

In the chaos, a new thought cut her like a knife. *Where are the two savages I tracked overhead?* Her insides went cold when Ash yelled, "They're digging at the ice! Von! They'll cause a blowout!"

She glanced up. The two males had grasped the cavern ceiling. They'd found seams with their pedicellaria, worming their arms deeper to create fissures and cracks, tugging in clockwise patterns.

Vonnie lunged. She grabbed one with each glove, crunching through the blunt horn-like spikes on their topsides. Two bulges of extra cartilage protected their brains. She squeezed. In a human, the result would have been spasms and unconsciousness. The sunfish went rigid, increasing their torque. They tore at the ice before she ripped them loose. She hurled them down in a shower of chunks and dust.

A breeze ruffled at the dust. Alarm bars filled her visor as the dust levitated, then swept upward through a few holes in the ceiling.

"I'm spraying emergency sealants!" Ben shouted.

"Von, our mecha are reinforcing the ice," Koebsch said. "We can stop the blowout. The tent contained most of it."

"I told you this would happen," Ash growled.

"The pressure held. You aren't losing atmosphere," Ben said.

Vonnie rose and advanced on the tribe. She was aware that she'd reverted to a human posture. Fine. Let the sunfish learn her true capabilities. Towering over them, she widened her spotlight, bathing them in its heat, splattering the males' blood through the light as she raised her fists and screamed: —*Are you animals or worthy allies?*

—*We are Mid Clan Six-Six!* they cried.

—*You are too close to the surface! Too close! If they dig apart the ice, there is only death for you! I will survive while you asphyxiate!*

The matriarchs screeched. Four of them leapt, including Charlotte. Vonnie swung and missed.

The matriarchs went over her, springing off the nearest wall. Goose bumps lifted the hair on the back of her neck. She was surrounded, but the matriarchs ignored her. They attended to the battered males. They pacified the males by herding them into pairs and applying pressure to their wounds.

One sprawled limply on the floor. Vonnie had squeezed too hard, rupturing his brain case. Charlotte touched his swollen body and shrieked: —*No life. He serves as food.*

—*Food!* they cried.

Without thinking, Vonnie exposed her revulsion. She turned to avoid the sight. Then she realized she'd shown weakness. A fresh jolt of adrenaline lit her veins and she rushed to place her back against the wall, certain they would attack.

The sunfish studied her in the echoing dark. Large or small, they'd paused as a single unit. They piped and screeched, measuring her.

—*Eat? Eat? Eat? Eat?* they cried.

Vonnie stood motionless. Her temples throbbed from the strain of gritting her teeth. With a soft *zzzzz*, the welding laser on her wrist went to full power.

Charlotte slashed at the dead male, cutting his belly with her beak. She popped him open with a familiar clockwise pull of her arms. Then she threw his entrails in a spiraling mess. The sunfish swarmed.

Breathing hard, Vonnie thought, *They wondered if I was claiming the first bite. My God. They expected me to lead them in their feast.*

Were they honoring me? Bowing to me? It's too much. I've learned so many things from them. I'm more committed and frank than ever, but this is too much. I can't pretend to eat with them. I won't.

"Von, are you okay?" Koebsch asked.

Ben said, "Your pulse and respiration are through the roof. Take it easy. You're not really down there, remember? You're safe in 06 with me."

"I remember."

"Someone else can take over if you want."

"Thank you. I'm okay," she said distantly, watching the sunfish gobble the male's softer parts. Others ripped at hunks of skin or rubbery strands of cartilage.

As her suit's radar targeting automatically tracked each sunfish in the crowd, another truth dawned on her. Lam and the matriarchs kept the savages from most of the warm flesh. Lam made no pretense of eating himself. He was simply an enforcer as the matriarchs devoured the best meat and innards. They allowed the few intelligent males like Tom to gorge as well, but the savages were given scraps.

More interesting, the larger breed didn't join the riot. They hung back, silently communicating among themselves with their arms.

Why hadn't they shoved into the blood y mess? Did they disapprove? What if the Mid Clans hadn't adopted the same necessary custom of devouring their own dead? Would they condemn the smaller sunfish and dissolve their alliance?

"Dawson is shouting at his display," Ben reported with an ugly laugh. "He must love this."

"Why do you say that?" Koebsch asked.

"Use your head," Ben said. "Cannibalism is exactly what he needs to make public opinion of the sunfish even worse. Are we editing our datastreams? Maybe we should."

"That's illegal," Koebsch said.

The two of them want to argue about everything, Vonnie thought. *Ben keeps needling him and Koebsch keeps asserting his authority just like the sunfish challenge each other.*

"We're more similar than we look," she murmured. She felt like the color was returning to her face. With it, her head cleared. She clicked on her radio and said, "Lam, what are the larger sunfish talking about?"

—*New sunfish eat. Old sunfish wait.*

"They're not angry with the smaller breed?"

—*No. Happy. New sunfish are hungry and sick. Need protein. Need oxygen.*

"They decided to let the smaller sunfish eat," O'Neal agreed. "A single corpse isn't much, and they want to improve the overall health of their new clan."

Vonnie nodded to herself, surprised and pleased. She hadn't anticipated such generosity. It boded well. If the larger breed lived in a rich environment, peace and wealth might explain their size. She began to ask if Lam had gleaned any clues about their home when he radioed again.

He seemed more lucid now. He used full sentences, perhaps he was replying to O'Neal, a biologist like the man he'd been. He said: —*The new clan also needs fewer savages. The larger sunfish were not upset when you killed one.*

"I wish I hadn't."

—*The matriarchs are working toward the same judgment. It's why they kept the savages from the most nutritious parts of the dead male. Instead, they allowed the savages to eat the cartilage and pedicellaria.*

"Lam, no. What judgment?"

—*They will kill others.*

"Tell them to stop!" she yelled. "We can't slaughter everyone who isn't smart enough."

—*You pushed them toward their decision.*

"Me? I didn't. Please. We can find roles for the smaller males. The tribe still needs workers and scouts."

—*They are animals. You asked if they're animals. You said animals will destroy the tribe, and the matriarchs heard your disapproval.*

"Wait!"

—*Do not interfere.*

"Von, we need to listen to him," O'Neal said.

"Our top priority is peace," Koebsch added. "If the matriarchs get rid of one or two of the worst males..."

"Jesus Christ, do you know what you're asking?"

"Affirmative," Koebsch said for the record. "Von, you've reminded us a thousand times how alien they are. You're also correct that they're a bit like us. Every day they compete among themselves. They want a chance to improve. That's what we offered them."

"We can't endorse murder," she said. She repeated her protests to the sunfish. —*Your smaller males are animals because of starvation and disease. Join us. My clan has endless food. We can make your eggs healthy again.*

The matriarchs screamed. They stroked the wounded males protectively, shielding them from Vonnie... but there was also melancholy in their body shapes.

—*The stupid males will always be stupid males*, Lam translated. —*They cannot change.*

"I can help them!"

—*The matriarchs do not want your help in dealing with the savage males. Their new clan has the warriors it needs in the larger sunfish. The healthy smaller males are superior scouts and hunters. Even without accepting an alliance with you, Mid Clan Six-Six has become a superior tribe. The savages are a liability.*

"My God, don't..."

—*This is what you asked for. Intelligence. Cooperation. Mid Clan Six-Six cannot adhere to your principles with the savages polluting their tribe.*

The many sunfish rearranged themselves. The matriarchs, their intelligent males and the larger breed pulled away from the scattered remains of the corpse.

The savages kept eating. That they'd been provided with a last meal was not due to fondness or compassion. The scraps were a diversion. As the savages bickered with each other, tussling over a few specks of flesh, the tribe encircled them.

"There has to be another way!" Vonnie shouted. She flexed her gloves, leaning toward the savages as if to defend them from the other sunfish.

—Do not interfere.

"Von, stay back," Koebsch said.

"We'll banish them!" Vonnie cried. She reached out to block Charlotte and Lam. "Don't kill them! Send them into the ice. Let them go. I demand it."

Two of the savages turned as if to look up. With preternatural speed, the others sensed the change in the first two. All seven of the savage males retreated into a clump like a phalanx, guarding each other.

Vonnie's subconscious must have known the result of her movements. She couldn't bear to witness a massacre, so she'd allowed the savages an advantage. They should have been defenseless. Instead, they'd recognized their tribemates' attack formation.

The matriarchs shrieked. Then the tribe fell upon the savage males. Charlotte bumped Vonnie's wrist as she leapt, thunking against her suit's plastisteel. The brief contact was menacing and insolent. *—Fight!* Charlotte screeched.

—Obey me! Vonnie cried.

Lam joined the matriarchs and the larger sunfish, leading with his metal arm. They immediately dominated the conflict, although they sustained blows and gashes they might have avoided if the savages hadn't been warned.

—Stop! Vonnie cried. *—Let them go!*

The paroxysm of beaks and arms intensified as the sunfish succumbed to their killing lust. Shadows flailed through Vonnie's spotlight, then sprays of blood and ice.

They chewed on each other. Screaming, touching, clasping

enemy and friend alike, they read each other. They knew their opponents' dying confusion. They shared their madness, their agony, their dreams and their plans.

The savages sprained a larger female's arm and lacerated Charlotte's topside. They bit another matriarch. Tom was injured above one ear. That was the extent of the fight. Within forty seconds, the savages were incapacitated or dead. Then the wounded were killed. A savage's tortured wail faded from the cavern as they eviscerated him.

Vonnie almost threw up. *No*, she thought, staring through a sticky dark mist of body fluids. The grisly fog wafted through the cavern on disturbed currents of air, then sank to the floor as it froze into red clots and snowflakes.

She shut her eyes.

"You're safe with me," Ben said. "Von, I'm right beside you in Module 06."

She might have nodded. She looked again. At her feet, the sunfish bolted down as much meat as they could cram into their stomachs. The larger breed ate, too. There was only a single monster who did not consume the dead. Lam.

"Why..." Vonnie said weakly.

—*They believed you were testing their resolve*, Lam told her. —*Their sole explanation that was you questioned their vows to accept your treaty. They killed their savages to bring harmony.*

"You helped them!" she said out of spite. "Don't say it's their fault. I watched you do it."

—*Yes. No. We killed the savages for you.*

Weeping, nodding, Vonnie offered a miserable prayer to whatever gods existed. She would never forgive herself. She had thought Dawson's betrayal of the ESA crew and Top Clan Eight-Six was appalling. Now the sunfish had betrayed their males for her.

They did it for me.

Far away, the ice was haunted by a shivering cry from the sunfish beneath the FNEE modules. Vonnie's suit modified the call into a long scream like a diving hawk. It was a song of violence and rapture.

In unison, the matriarchs and the larger sunfish drew their beaks from the corpses. Wet with grotesque, steaming innards, they screeched. —*Danger! Kill!*

Vonnie raised her welding laser and pressed closer to the wall. Her body felt like a coiled wire until O'Neal spoke.

"Don't show fear," he said.

She reset herself. She took a new, lower shape by kneeling on the ice, but she kept her laser up. She expected the sunfish to come for her next. Their execution of the males went against everything she'd imagined for them. Beside it, Dawson's betrayal seemed insignificant, and the males' deaths had been her fault. She'd betrayed herself.

Caught between the cavern wall and the shrieking matriarchs, Vonnie called desperately on her radio to Lam. "What do they want?" she asked.

—*You won't like it*, he said.

"Tell me."

—*The sunfish below the FNEE are enacting the same purge. They are also killing their savages.*

11.

Vonnie staggered in relief and new fear. The matriarchs weren't screaming at her. They were calling *through* her. They'd ordered a new slaughter across the ice.

Ribeiro broke into her audio feed by issuing a Class 1 alert, his voice thick with repugnance. "A bloodbath is underway in the fractures beneath us," he said. "The larger sunfish have attacked the smaller kind."

Vonnie shook off her paralysis. "You're wrong," she said. "It's both breeds against a specific group of smaller males, isn't it?"

Ribeiro deflected any admission of a mistake. "Our systems are tracking more than forty individual combatants in a congested space," he said. "A few were lost beneath an ice fall. Others are already dead."

"Koebsch, it's a disaster," Henri said. He was in the FNEE command module with Ribeiro and used the same emergency channel.

Vonnie was preoccupied with the sunfish in her cavern. They had resumed their feast and she stayed back with her laser up, salvaging her thoughts from her own turmoil. "The sunfish don't care about you," she said.

"They may bring down our modules," Ribeiro said.

"Colonel, check your systems and our transcripts again," Koebsch said. "The intelligent sunfish are killing the savages. They want to accept our treaty."

"What they want is immaterial if collateral damage opens a

hole in the ice," Ribeiro said.

"Stand down," Koebsch said. "Do not send our mecha through the lock. Do not activate our weapon systems. Is that clear?"

"Affirmative."

"Sir, their fight is over," Tavares reported. Vonnie brightened at the young sergeant's voice. "Some of the larger breed are shoring up the wall that collapsed," Tavares said. "Others are digging through the debris."

"That's good news," Koebsch said.

"It does not look like good news," Ribeiro said. "They are eating their dead. How do we know they won't begin a new fight when they require their next meal?"

"That's unlikely," Koebsch said. "The purge wasn't motivated by hunger."

"Ash, please check our grid," O'Neal said. "Ribeiro told us some of the sunfish were lost. Are they buried or did they get away?"

"They got away," Ash said. "I show three radar signatures moving northeast from the FNEE modules at a depth of point zero two klicks. They're not coming toward us."

"I wasn't worried about three savages attacking our camp, but it may affect how the Mid Clan deals with us if a few of their undesirables escaped," O'Neal said. "Von, you need to keep that in mind as you talk to them."

Vonnie spoke like she was in a nightmare, forcing each word through her disbelief. "You want us to hunt them down?"

"I want us to remove rival hunters or saboteurs from the area and have the bodies to prove our success," O'Neal said. "I want us to look invincible."

"How did this happen?" she asked. "Now we're killing sunfish in order to save them?"

"Von, it's who they are." O'Neal was gentle, but what she noticed was the conspicuous silence of Ben and Koebsch. Maybe it was better for her relationship with each man that she didn't shout at them.

On the cavern floor, the matriarchs and the larger sunfish finished eating, although two of the dead males were mostly intact. Their oozing blood had been lapped up. Then their shredded organs were repacked and their injuries were sloshed with urine, which froze, sealing them shut. Both corpses would be preserved for later.

Meanwhile, the living sunfish picked at their tribemates, removing every fleck of gore from their skins and their stubby defensive spikes.

The two breeds crawled among each other indiscriminately. The slaughter had done more than remove an irritant. It had served as a marriage. Charlotte, Lam, and four larger females formed a nucleus at the bottom of their heap, a new arrangement of leaders... and Vonnie saw their nucleus was composed of six instead of a more typical quartet.

Was that relevant to the tribe's new name?

As the leaders directed their beaks at Vonnie, they sent Tom and Brigit and two larger males to the cavern ceiling, dividing the pack so that nearly half of them took submissive positions above her.

—*We are Six-Six!* they cried.

Vonnie shifted her weight as she studied them, acknowledging the changes in the group; their losses; their improved balance and strength. But she wondered if Ribeiro's pessimism was correct. Had they proclaimed a death sentence on the savages partly because of their hunger?

The new leaders noticed the misgivings in her. They replied with their own suspicion. —*How does Ghost Clan live beyond the ice?* Charlotte called.

—*You know we have metal like the shape I wear or like him*, Vonnie said with a gesture at Lam. Feeling like she was on safe ground as they discussed engineering and ROM, she grew more confident. —*We have tools beyond your knowledge, and we can build farms and reservoirs for you. We can make good atmosphere. We will share.*

—*Ghost Clan will fight for Mid Clan?*

Vonnie hesitated, but she didn't need to ask Koebsch how he would respond. A bureaucrat would compromise. An administrator would accept some evil for the greater good. She was repelled by the idea of killing more sunfish to preserve one clan, but she nodded. —*Yes*, she said.

They screamed in triumph when she gave her oath. —*We would be Thirty with you!* they shrieked.

—*We are Twenty-Sixteen!* she cried. She wasn't sure what they wanted. "O'Neal, Charlotte said that before. 'We would be Thirty with you.' Do you know what she means?"

"It's not a sunfish number," O'Neal said. "I think it's how they envision a union with us."

"A new number," she said.

Maybe, just maybe, the bloodshed had been worth uniting the two breeds. She was cheered by the prospect of teaching them. Someday the sunfish might achieve more unity than humankind had ever learned. Caught in the frozen sky, unable to leave its dwindling resources, their tribes had more incentive to work together than the widespread cultures on Earth.

Achieving such a goal would require years or decades. First they needed someone to show the way.

She let them sense her eagerness. She adjusted her body from a closed posture to an inviting one. She opened her arms. She lifted her head. But there was also a trace of caution in how she remained apart from the tribe with her back against the cavern wall.

—*Thirty is an unknown sum,* she said. —*Explain it to me. The savages are gone. Who are you?*

—*We are Six-Six!* the leaders cried.

Vonnie knew this was more than a rote answer. She struggled to read as much into their calls and body language as they intended. At the same time, her visor filled with extrapolations and sims.

Their name was their totality. To the sunfish, *Six-Six* defined equilibrium. It described a fundamental vitality and right-mindedness. They were self-assured to the point of arrogance. They found her caution aggravating, but they slowed themselves to match her pace. They demonstrated their worth by holding themselves in check.

They bragged to her.

—*We know the top and the middle,* they cried. —*We have touched the bottom.*

—*What is there? What is there?* she asked.

They shrugged off her question and boasted again. —*We can rule the ice with you. We are healthy and fertile and smart.*

—*Healthy, yes. A treaty, yes.*

—*We deliver ourselves to you as equals. Our strength is yours and yours is ours.*

—*Not yet,* she said. —*Many of your tribe aren't here. My clan sees them in the ice to the northeast. Who speaks for them? Do those sunfish accept your choice?*

—*Yes! Yes!*

Charlotte and Lam screamed at the cavern floor with the larger females. His voice was so high-pitched, he would have torn his larynx if it was flesh. The larger females chorused with him, guiding his meaning, adding to his volume.

He shook the ice.

Far away, the other sunfish replied: —*Yes! Yes! We are Six-Six!*

Her radio chattered with human voices. "There is another commotion beneath our modules," Ribeiro barked.

"Colonel, it's okay," O'Neal said. "Both groups of sunfish are negotiating the terms of an alliance with us."

"Administrator Koebsch, I cannot permit the presence of an uncontrolled native force beneath our living quarters," Ribeiro said.

"We'll ask them to move," Vonnie said, feeling awestruck again at their abilities.

Forever blind, forever scuttling through the three-dimensional maze of their world, the sunfish were uniquely qualified to act in concert with each other. Their group mind extended across short distances. Every leader spoke for the rest.

—*Bring your entire tribe to me,* she cried. —*Call them to this cavern. We will eat. We will rest. I can help your injured and your sick.*

—They will come. Your kind comes, too?

—Yes. More suits, more mecha, she cried. To her radio, she said, "Ash, on my mark, can you send tools and food into the cargo tube?"

"Roger that."

The sunfish churned around Vonnie. They shrieked with new enthusiasm, and Ben said, "I'm reading a Class 3 alarm from our seismographs. They're affecting the cavern ceiling again, although it's not bad. Not yet."

—Calm, calm, Vonnie cried. *—Sing quietly.*

—A quiet song. Yes. No. Yes, they called.

Long after the fact, it occurred to her that Lam's wavering might not represent schizophrenia. The sunfish thought in darts and jolts. Each idea ping-ponged among them until they found consensus. Did that mean Lam was more sane than she'd worried?

The tribe slithered. They called and danced, repeating her promises of medicine and food.

"The sunfish beneath the FNEE modules are on the move," Ben reported. "They're descending into the ice. Von, they're heading toward you. Time of arrival is seven minutes."

"Nice work," Koebsch said.

Vonnie would have liked to scoff at Ribeiro, but nothing good could come from publicly raking him over the coals. If she wanted to reach an accord with him, or, less likely, bring him to her cause, she needed to let him win a few rounds. *Maybe he can hunt the savages for us*, she thought. He was a soldier. He should be able to relate to the tribe's security concerns.

While the sunfish screamed at their approaching kin, Vonnie

switched radio links and spoke privately to Lam. "Thank you for your help. I mean it. We couldn't have come this far without you."

—*New tribe*, he said. —*Good tribe*.

"Lam, can I do something to help you?" she asked. "We could fix your mem files. We could repair your arm."

—*No. No. Yes. No.*

Faced with his inhuman dilemma, she hurried to explain. "Your arm is a sign of strength and you're one of them now. Everyone can see that. If you're okay, we don't have to talk about it. But I want to help. If you need anything..."

—*Yes. No. No. No.*

"All right. I can give you more capacity if you change your mind. I can run corrective sequences if you decide you want them. We owe you. Everyone up here is in your debt. So is the tribe."

—*Thank you. No. No.*

There wasn't time to push Lam. She needed to increase the bonds between their species. She wanted to introduce Charlotte to the varied personalities who'd supported her, so she sent five alerts to Ben, Harmeet, Ash, O'Neal and Koebsch. "Let me have audio from the group feed, please," she said. "You can keep my station quarantined if you're still concerned about a cyber attack from Lam, but I want to share your voices with the tribe."

"Roger that," Koebsch said.

Shutting off her spotlight, Vonnie walked into the throng of sunfish. She invited them closer by opening her arms. —*These are my people*, she cried before she said, "I'm mingling with the tribe. Their affirmation ritual might take a while, and I need to pay attention to them, but I want you to know I'm proud to serve with you."

"My pleasure, Von," Koebsch said.

Her speakers conveyed his sincerity through the cavern. The sunfish jerked in surprise, then chirped their approval.

Ben's voice held an edge. He pretended he was relaxed, but Vonnie heard his wariness toward Koebsch. So did the sunfish, who tensed. "Hey, it's been fun so far," Ben said. "I wouldn't miss it."

"I could have skipped some parts," Ash said, a rare joke for her.

Vonnie grinned. "Me too."

—*Ghosts!* the sunfish cried. —*We hear Ghosts!*

She'd counted on their wonder and excitement. Encouraging them to learn was her best defense against men like Dawson.

Then her grin faded. Despite everything, she was stunned when the sunfish launched into a detailed analysis of her crewmates. Tom led the tribe through several parts of their new song by adding personal cues. —*[First voice/Koebsch] is your dominant male. [Second voice/Ben] is your current mate. [Third voice/Ash] is a rival female, fertile and aggressive. [Koebsch] seeks to lead us and protect you. We will listen. We will listen. [Ben] challenges him. [Ash] challenges you.*

"Oh, uh," Vonnie said.

"That's ridiculous," Ash said. She was flustered like Vonnie, but Ben laughed.

"They're not far off the mark," he said.

"How can they know so much?" Koebsch asked, although their skills had been proven weeks ago.

Their hyper-sensitivity allowed them to track the behavior of every human on the surface. Tom had also heard radio exchanges inside 07, and other scouts must have intercepted the faintest vibrations of conversations inside their hab modules.

Attempting to hide from the tribe was pointless.

—*I will show you more of us,* Vonnie cried. "Harmeet? O'Neal?" she asked.

Harmeet took her motherly stance, not solely for Vonnie but also for the sunfish. She complimented them. "You performed very well today," she said.

"Von, the other group will reach you in two minutes," O'Neal said. He was all business, and Vonnie felt glad again at his unflappable nature. O'Neal was a rock. He was exactly the kind of man who should have been sent to deal with aliens, not shitheads like Dawson.

—*More voices?* the sunfish cried. —*We want more voices.*

—*These are my people,* Vonnie said. She'd hoped to focus on her supporters, not anyone who might persuade the sunfish to decline a treaty. Had they sensed her thoughts about Dawson in her body language?

—*We know [Fourth voice/Harmeet],* they cried. —*We know [Fifth voice/O'Neal]. She is a matriarch. He serves as an advisor. Like you, [O'Neal] and [Ben] guide your clan's metal scouts.*

"That's impossible," Ash said. "They can't tell who operates the mecha."

—*[Ash] challenges us like she challenges you! [Ash] is young. She is <striking prey>. She also guides your scouts when you allow her.*

"They're guessing," Ash said. She was unnerved.

Ben spoke with conviction. "No," he said. "I believe it."

"Any pilot will tell you ships fly differently with different people at the controls," Vonnie said. "Ash, you know that's true. It's not always obvious, but you can see changes in how the same mecha act if Ben or Ribeiro is in charge."

—Where are [Loud Warrior] and [Shy Foot] and [Quick Walk]? the sunfish cried. —Where is [Old Foe]?

"'Old Foe' is Dawson," O'Neal said.

"How did they learn about him?" Koebsch asked.

"Look at his name," O'Neal said. "They've described him by his relationship with Von even though all of us have butted heads with him. 'Loud Warrior' is Ribeiro. I think the others are Tavares and Henri."

'Shy Foot,' Vonnie thought. That's a superficial description of Tavares, but Henri moves expertly in everything he does. 'Quick Walk' sounds like him.

"Hold on," Ben objected. "Your transcripts referred to the rest of us 'First voice' or 'Second voice.'"

"The AIs were still working on their translations," O'Neal said.

Ben laughed. "So let's hear it, man! What do they call Koebsch?"

"His name means something like 'Mature Male,'" O'Neal said. "They don't have a word for 'Patriarch,' but that's the connotation. Vitality. Leadership."

"Mm." Ben must have hoped they'd given Koebsch a disparaging term like 'Old Boss' or 'Timid Male.'

O'Neal seemed oblivious to Ben's botched attempt to put his rival in a bad light. Reading from his displays, O'Neal was as captivated as a child with a mirror. "Harmeet is 'Elder Matriarch,'" he said. "I'm 'Wise Scout.' Von is 'Young Matriarch.' Ben, you're 'Biting Male' and Ash has same primary feature of 'Biting Female.' The implication is a contrary member of our crew."

"Got it," Ben said. He didn't want to hear more.

Vonnie muffled her laughter. Maybe it was perverse, but she found Ben especially loveable when he tripped himself up. It made him more human. Like her. She'd made more errors than she could count.

Meanwhile, the sunfish had continued their song. As they chorused and danced, hammering through what they'd learned, one new thread of information emerged.

—*We hear your strength*, they cried. —*We know your many kinds. We are a conglomeration like you!*

Then their song accelerated. They became a tapestry of names. They overwhelmed the AIs, and O'Neal stammered in his delight. "They... They're describing our mecha!" he said. "Tiny spies. Small beacons. Diggers. Rovers. Listening posts."

"The rovers are above the surface," Ash protested. Now her tone was more than unnerved. She sounded stiff with fear.

"They're describing our modules and landers, too," O'Neal said. "The sheds. The tents. Our jeeps and scout suits."

Vonnie had stopped feeling astonished. She realized she was grinning again like a loon. "Imagine what it's like to live with so many connections. They hear so clearly. They'll make better scouts than anything we can build."

"I may have some bad news," Koebsch said. "Von, radar shows forty-two survivors in the approaching group. That's a lot."

"They're going to fill the cavern," Ben said.

"They'll bury you! I couldn't stand it if I..." Ash caught herself. "Take me off speaker."

"Ash, no," Vonnie said. "Don't go away. We don't want anyone to withdraw. This openness is normal for them. They share everything."

"I don't like it."

"Do you feel like they're spying on you?" Vonnie asked. Mostly she was teasing. She also hoped she'd stung Ash, the British mole, but the young woman missed the irony.

"They *are* spying on us," Ash said. "They've mapped everything. Look at O'Neal's transcripts. Their names for us include specific locations in camp. They even know we're not in the same modules."

"We've mapped them, too," Ben said. "I don't see how this changes anything."

"I hate to say it, but Ben is right," Koebsch said. "Von, keep going. You have forty seconds before the bigger group arrives."

Vonnie selected five recommendations from her AI. —*Your ears are wise*, she called. —*You know us well. We have many kinds, many strengths. We blend our varied shapes into one potent clan.*

—*Many strengths!* the sunfish cried.

"Good. Perfect," O'Neal said. "Looks at my sims and the AI's projections. During that last song, the tribe kept repeating their shapes for 'conglomeration.' I think they were doing more than listing our different mecha and people. They compared Lam and their two breeds with our group. They're trying to say they could fit in, too."

"Then she's done it," Ben said. "We're on the verge of a treaty with them."

"Nice work," Koebsch said for the second time.

Vonnie shook her head. "It was you, too. It was everyone. If we hadn't..."

The ice crackled with the oncoming weight of sunfish. "Here we go," Koebsch said. The bigger group shoved up through the maze as Vonnie greeted them, matching their cries with her own. —*We are here! We are here! We are here! We are here!*

The sunfish billowed through the cavern like muscular confetti, dodging among each other, screeching in an unusual hush. They jostled her with their many arms.

As they brushed against her, the AIs translated their tone as respectful, even reverent. "They're waiting for your signal," O'Neal said. "They want your affirmation."

"Koebsch, would you like to take over the suit?" Vonnie asked. "You're our 'Mature Male.' You should be the one who tells them."

"Absolutely not," he said. "They should hear from 'Young Matriarch.' You've earned it."

"Thank you. All of you."

Her crewmates had been amazing. Over dinner, O'Neal might get a kiss. So would Koebsch — a chaste, sisterly peck — and Ben was in for a thorough lovemaking on her bunk.

Vonnie smiled at her to-do list. She snickered out loud when the sunfish perceived her exultation.

Their treaty had been written in the blood of the smaller males, but it was more concrete due to their sacrifice. Her guilt, her faith, her fascination with Europa and her drive to solve its mysteries, each of these emotions added fuel to the obligation she felt not only to the sunfish but to her friends.

They deserved more appreciation than she could express. Later, she would hug everyone from Henri to Harmeet... everyone except Dawson. She intended to curse the old bastard like she'd wanted to yell at Ribeiro. In fact, Dawson would get a double dose since she knew she'd never win his support whereas Ribeiro might come around eventually. He took honor in his service. If she could convince him that the sunfish were unparalleled allies, would he see them in a new light?

As for she and Ben and Koebsch, they needed to figure out their triangle, an extremely un-sunfish-like predicament.

She also planned to buy Ash a drink. Maybe they could become buddies again. Europa was too cold to stand apart from another woman close to her own age.

In coming days, she would also have time to scrutinize and repair Lam as they explored the ice. They would develop the enormous potential of the union between the two breeds and humankind. Soon they would approach neighboring clans. She hoped to spend the rest of her life on this incredible moon.

We'll make it work, she thought.

The sunfish felt her confidence. Their movements were relaxed as they bumped against each other, burying Submodule 07, clinging to the ice.

At the base of the densely packed crowd, Vonnie sang. She told them what she believed her friends were thinking. —*We are pleased to join with you. Our tribe is your tribe.*

—*We are Thirty!* the sunfish cried.

—*Yes.* Vonnie cradled eight of them in her arms, increasing their physical contact. Tom hung on her shoulder. Lam called from nearby, offering a more reserved link with her as Charlotte and three larger females seized her leg.

Their weight would have been too much for a person without a scout suit. With it, Vonnie held them easily, demonstrating yet again the power they craved. The sunfish called and danced, celebrating.

Vonnie smiled.

—*We are Ghost Clan Thirty!* she cried.

NOT THE END

Acknowledgments

More of the usual suspects participated in the writing of *Betrayed*; Ben Bowen, Ph.D., computational biologist with Lawrence Berkeley National Laboratory; Charles H. Hanson, M.D.; my father, Gus Carlson, Ph.D., mechanical engineer and former division leader with Lawrence Livermore National Laboratory; Matthew J. Harrington, evil genius, author of many of the stories in the *Man-Kzin War* collections and co-author of *The Goliath Stone*; Penny Hill, who's just a boring old regular genius; and keen-eyed Grampy Lee Ashford.

The talented Jasper Schreurs put together another killer cover, bringing Vonnie to life. The man who should land on Europa himself as part of the ESA engineering crew, Jeff Sierzenga, devised the maps and schematics throughout the novel.

Without these people, the Europa Series would not exist. Some of them were given beer and sandwiches. Others have been written into my books. All of them deserve my thanks.

You guys rock.

Jeff
jeff@jverse.com

If you liked *BETRAYED*...

LOOK FOR THE BESTSELLING NOVELS BY JEFF CARLSON

"Terrifying."
—Scott Sigler, *New York Times* bestselling author of *Pandemic*

"Edgy and exciting."
—Bob Mayer, *New York Times* bestselling author of the *Green Berets* and *Area 51* series.

The next breath you take will kill you.

"Part Michael Crichton, part George Romero...
full of high-altitude chills."
—E. E. Knight

"A grim and fascinating new twist on
the post-holocaust story."
—Kevin J. Anderson

JEFF CARLSON

From the *Long Eyes* collection… the original short story of…

"Interrupt"

Whatever happened to the sun seems to be intensifying. This time I blacked out for at least five days — I haven't grown so much beard since I was seventeen. Jan would have been shocked. It's shaved now. I managed a quick sponge bath, too. Jan ridiculed me for being "an anal robot" but keeping clean might be the only way to mark the length of each interrupt. I can't trust myself not to lose this journal, or start a fire with its pages. I think we're still smart enough to use tools.

These notes can't be my first attempt to document the phenomenon, but none of the laptops will even boot up. Electromagnetic pulses strong enough to affect our brains might have fried every computer chip on the planet. Wolsinger's mini-D was on my desk with a fresh disc in it, half recorded, but the playback is badly garbled.

Have I already tried to build a shield? That was my first thought now. It was probably my first thought before. How else to explain the trash heap of metal in the cafeteria? Pots, pans, garbage cans, the hoods of the truck and the jeep.

How many times have I already failed? With only a limited ability to form short-term memories, I could waste my lucid periods attempting the same thing over and over and over.

~ ~ ~

Not much to do now except write to stay awake. I don't know if I could sleep anyway, give up my conscious mind voluntarily. I'm dizzy, though. Blisters on my thumb. I'd like to wash again, get off the stink of hard labor and, yes, the reek of fear, but I'm still dehydrated from tramping around in the heat all day and the cafeteria tanks are nearly empty. The pumps aren't working, of course. And I have to conserve in case I'm trapped.

In a while I'll patrol the front again but I think they went away. It's a good thing the building's concrete or they might have tried to burn me out. The locals must think we're doing this to them, all those antennas and the dish array. No need to speak Spanish to understand. I've never seen such hatred, not even in Jan after our court battles. The people here were always suspicious, I guess, no matter if we paid well in hard American dollars or gave away our medical supplies. Most of them have tried all their lives to get out of here, tried for generations, yet in comes a pack of gringo Dr. Frankensteins like the jungle was a petting zoo, blabbering about new laser spectrometers and listening for people in the stars. And I am a gringo here, no matter that my skin is darker than theirs.

Why did they come up the hill this evening? Because they heard me tinkering and were afraid I'd unleash another interrupt? I wish I was a better shot. I only tried to wound that stupid loudmouth when he grabbed me.

The moon is quarter full and waxing. Last I remember it was August 16th but it may be September already. So near the equator there are no real seasons, and the constellations don't move half as much as when I was a boy much further north. The stars seem to say it's October but that can't be right.

My old friends look cold and ugly tonight, glittering wildly like polished flecks of bone. What pressure storms are surging through the upper atmosphere?

There's no way to build a shield. I wrote that on the wall in magic marker, just to be safe. Have to stop wasting time on the idea. If I had machining tools it would be different. If I wasn't alone. If I wasn't on this goddamn rock in the middle of nowhere. There's definitely enough metal to line the cafeteria walls and ceiling, armor it thick and deep, if I could dismantle the jeep and the truck and the panels of the main dish, make sheeting out of the fenders, cut and bend everything to fit, flatten every fuel drum and computer and appliance in this place.

If... if... if...

If this was one of those idiotic monster movies Blair insisted on playing every time it was his night to choose a DVD, we could probably wrap our heads in tinfoil and be safe. Metal umbrellas. The fence might have been easiest to mold into a shield, but the holes in the chain link are huge in comparison to most wavelengths in the solar spectrum — too much would pass. I considered a body suit or even just a spherical helmet made of interwoven layers of window screens, but this building has plastic filament instead of metal, rust-proof.

I have another plan. An EM cone. I should be able to pull Dish 4 off the tower, rewire it to transmit. If I can generate a broadcast of matching amplitude and frequencies, precisely out of phase, I can neutralize the interrupt phenomenon locally. But I'll need power and working electronics.

~ ~ ~

Morning. It's stayed quiet. If Wolsinger and Blair are still in the area, I hope they'll avoid the locals.

Scott McCay is dead. He has been for at least a week by the look of him, though it's tough to judge given the condition of his body. There also are dead or feeble lizards and snakes everywhere. Something in their physiology. The birds are having a field day, feasting — but they're flying a bit unsteadily, I think. Maybe only deep-water life forms are completely unaffected. People in submarines and bomb shelters.

It's ironic that the next interrupt may actually help us. The locals might not decide we're at fault the next time they're lucid, if another flare hits soon enough. The brain requires days to fully absorb and organize new memories, and that process is being disrupted.

How?

Normal solar radiation can reach microscopic lengths on the nanometer scale and smaller, though the atmosphere typically deflects EM of these wavelengths — and the synaptic gap ranges between 30 and 40nm.

Extreme flares must be overriding our bioelectric processes, like white noise. But if it's interfering with our ability to think, why aren't we left twitching and drooling on the ground? Or maybe we are. Maybe at times we're completely incapacitated. Sudden collapses might explain the bruises on my hip and chest, the abrasion on my cheek.

Unless I got hurt fighting.

I found McCay near the wooden shack that we paid the locals to put up for a garage, his skull smashed. Something had been eating at his neck and belly but I left him there. Securing the generators took first priority. All eight were already topped off and someone had taken steps to reinforce the surrounding fence. Me? Someone unused to that kind of labor — a sloppy but effective job of stringing razor wire and chaining the downhill corner that always sagged. Extra fuel had been siphoned from the drums in the garage.

The garage. Was McCay trying to leave? I assumed at first that Wolsinger and Blair had wandered off in a delirium during the last interrupt. Where is there to escape to? Could we have had a plan, received a radio message?

No matter how long I concentrate, I can't summon more than a few random images of the past days, and it's all confused with my long-term memories of this place. Finding food must be our main focus. I remember hunger and base gratification. But there is also frustration and fear. Could I be aware, however faintly, of being mentally stunted? Do I search and search for what's been stolen from me? For months after Jan left I felt like every organ in my body was packed with gravel, but this is horror on another scale — decay, repeated death.

If it continues, I suppose we may begin to lose our established memories as well. The brain is a lot like a computer. These constant shocks can't be healthy. I'm going to seal this journal in a waterproof CD-ROM container and chain it to my wrist.

~ ~ ~

Eating lunch in the shade of the dish array, greasy canned stew. The roof is like a stove top. The heat started my head thumping an hour ago and it's not even noon. I feel like I've been working here forever. My time sense doesn't seem completely reliable anymore. At least my coordination's still good. I ripped the guts out of Dish 1. The spectrometers were designed to withstand the EM fields generated by our own equipment, and over-engineered like most of our toys. They should still work.

Had to stop and write down what's happened in case there's another interrupt. I used two more bullets in the pistol this morning. The body of the loudmouth was gone, dragged away, and three people I vaguely recognized came out of the jungle — a scrawny old goat rancher flanked by his daughter and son. A year ago during the meet-and-greets, the same trio stood in the same formation, always in the very back, murmuring among themselves, the son too angry.

Today they were armed with gardening tools, and the rancher's hoe had gummy blood stains on it. That shouldn't have relieved me, but I was glad to know I wasn't the one who killed McCay. I fired over their heads and they ran. I've wasted every other minute since the looking behind me, listening, waiting for a rifle shot and sudden agony. Stupid bastards.

If I am the one who took care of the generators, that must be as far as I got last time. If I—

~ ~ ~

There was another interrupt, a brief one. I'm sure it's the same day because the canned stew I was eating has drawn a knot of flies but isn't baked hard yet. And no beard. It was incredibly strange reading over this journal. I am a stranger to that earlier self. How many times have I felt orphaned, doomed? Now at least I have this signpost. This bible.

I became a thinking human again at the far edge of the roof, pacing, the sun dropped low enough to stare me right in the face. My teeth ached from chewing on the chain around my wrist, like a dog. What if the interrupt had lasted longer? Would I have jumped eventually, two stories or not? Starved? Or could I have figured out how to open the stairwell?

I sat there and cried for twenty minutes.

Pulling the spectrometers is only the beginning. I'll need a functioning computer to regulate my broadcast, and an auto switch to stop and start it in time with the flares. Otherwise I'll simply blast myself with an interrupt of my own making. And of course one dish won't be enough. I have to produce a second EM cone to protect the generators or else they'll fry while producing the current I need. I suppose I could live on top of them, under the same dish, but then I'd need to construct a shelter and run water from the building...

My safe zone will be small, no wider than the dish and maybe ten feet long, room for a few people and supplies.

Please let this work.

~ ~ ~

Wolsinger's gone crazy. He got into the building without me noticing and I almost shot him. The sun had set and he was only a shadow, and he didn't answer when I shouted. He didn't even look up from his desk. I asked where he'd been, if he was okay. He just sat there holding his armrests like he was afraid he'd float away. When he did talk, his voice never rose above a mumble. I actually laughed at first. I thought he was saying that the villagers were doing this to us, until I realized he meant a different "they" altogether.

He said it was in our recordings, a carrier wave from somewhere in Epsilon Eridani. We didn't remember because the aliens didn't want us to. They were making the sun pulse in an abnormal pattern, blinding us, destroying us.

I spent an hour digging through our printouts to prove him wrong. There was no signal. There was nothing. Wolsinger didn't help, just sat there holding onto his chair and shaking his head. He said the computer records would show it if the aliens hadn't burned out our hard drives. He said he remembered.

I need his help, his hands. He said yes. Can I trust him?

His eyes are too large, red, always blinking. I made sure to keep the pistol out of his reach. Delusional paranoia. It has to be. Something in his brain. Even if he had seen an extraterrestrial message before the first interrupt, he couldn't know now. What's happening is a natural occurrence.

Humankind has always studied the sun, hoping to interpret the moods of the gods, and we know from ancient writings that our star has roiled and flared for millennia. An uncontained hydrogen reactor of such enormous scale could hardly be expected to do otherwise. Modern civilization with all its tools and sciences rapidly added to that knowledge, measuring random eruptions and re-cording a phenomenon known as solar maximum: extreme flares that occurred roughly every eleven years.

We assumed it had been happening like clockwork forever. But we only truly became aware of the phenomenon after we had power grids and communications to be disrupted — little more than a century. A hundred years is less than a blink in the life of the sun, and all of human history is hardly more.

It did seem as if each maximum came a bit sooner and did worse damage than the previous one, yet the few people who sounded an alarm were dismissed as nuts, Chicken Littles. Of course each max seemed worse. Each decade we had more satellites and technology to be affected. No one worried much.

The maximums must have been a recent instability. Earth's magnetosphere and ionosphere are obviously being wildly compressed and distorted, allowing exceptional amounts of EM to strike the planet's surface. The sun may be older than we assumed. We are still only guessing about so much of astrophysics. And if it is pre-nova, the onslaught of particle radiation may continue until it ultimately explodes in ten thousand years. Or this could simply be a natural period of adjustment, "blowing steam," as the sun stabilizes itself.

The lizards and snakes I've seen dead or crippled — cold-blooded life everywhere must be affected in the same way, except the amphibians capable of hiding underwater.

Maybe now we know what happened to the dinosaurs, and why only frogs and turtles still survive from those days. Crocodiles. Sharks and fish.

Maybe we're re-entering a phase of solar activity that kept complex brain function from arising for eons, which is why early humans appear to have been stuck in a series of long evolutionary ruts despite having a skull capacity equal to ours.

I've read enough anthropology to know it's the big question. Why did we take so long to become what we are today? For uncounted millennia we were brutes, with only the most simple tools and societies, and then in the space of four thousand years we built empires and cities and blanketed the entire planet with electricity and highways and super-agriculture. Maybe those few thousand years were an unusually quiet time for the sun. Maybe there were other bits of peace here and there, just enough for us to evolve as far as we did.

If so, my EM cone will be a very temporary solution, even if I had unlimited fuel. Maybe Wolsinger and I can rig a portable model on the jeep, locate more supplies, reach the caves in the mountains to the south. I can't see them but I know they're there, sixty or seventy miles by road. Central America is just one big spine of rock.

What's left of the human race will have to go underground, deep down, become moles and morlocks. Give up the stars, the sky, the rain and trees and everything we've ever known.

~ ~ ~

Remember this. Remember it always.

Your name is Roell Washington Carver Lloyd. You were born on July 21, 1969, just a day after a human being first walked on the face of the moon. Your mother, Marilyn, was forever proud of that. None of your professional accomplishments meant so much to her. Even as cancer ate out her bowels she still bragged to you, to her nurses, to other patients, that you had been a moon baby. She made you feel special. She wanted to name you Apollo or

Armstrong or even Rocket, but your father said those were white names. His name was Ed, which he hated. White as can be. He wasn't so proud of you for being book-smart. He wanted you tougher, better at sports, and made you waste a million after-noons throwing balls and bouncing balls and running with balls. But he raised you well enough, you and your sister Korba, in Richmond, California, which is very very far from here.

Too far to walk.

Too—

If I forget all of that I probably won't remember how to read, either, so what's the point?

~ ~ ~

I think eight days have passed since I wrote anything. My beard growth fits that time and the moon is going on full now. I found the generators rigged to come on one after another as they run out of fuel, and the last two are equipped with big auxiliary tanks. A stranger that was me had calculated their running time in grease pencil on the side of the last tank — eight hundred hours, roughly thirty days, somewhat less depending on how much power I use drawing water from the well.

A heavy-duty power line was strung from the generators to the cafeteria, where the first dish was bolted to the wall and floor. I suppose mounting it on the ceiling was too much, and it doesn't matter. The EM cone can be pointed in any direction. But I still haven't cobbled together a working computer. I found several PCs pulled apart beside the crude shell of the jeep's hood. Looks like another interrupt caught me in mid-task, and probably burned out everything I'd salvaged. They're coming more often and lasting longer now.

I woke in a protected corner of the cafeteria near the water tanks, in a crude nest of blankets, surrounded by fruit and some of those meaty leaves the size of my head. And I had what must be a weapon. A metal table leg. The pistol is gone. I think I was dreaming of Jan.

Once upon a time I enjoyed solitude, the peace and clarity of my work, but even Wolsinger would be a happy sight now. Maybe he won't be crazy this time. I've never been this alone before. I talk just to hear a voice.

Obviously I don't fully understand yet what we may or may not be capable of during the interrupts. The memory was so vivid, I could almost smell her.

~ ~ ~

Your wife Janice grew up an inner-city black, poor, exposed to gangs and drugs, but she had more style than an egghead from Cal Tech could ever quantify. You made a great team. She was popular, graceful and pretty, sometimes even stunning in the right dress. You gave her structure, paid the bills on time, remembered anniversaries. For a while that was enough.

It wasn't that you took her for granted — you were simply miserable at some of the things she needed, crowds, dancing, chitchat. And you were discovering new miracles every day that transported you twenty or fifty or a hundred and fifty light-years away. You made the safe choice, stuck with the things you understood, and eventually she left you for it.

Janice is probably dead. Things must be impossibly bad in urbanized areas.

Uncontrolled fires would barely be the beginning, entire cities roasting alive. Not enough food to go around. No water. And San Francisco already had its share of brutes and killers before people lost the ability to reason.

She might have been here with you and had some chance at survival if you'd been a better husband.

Survival. No one is going to live to a ripe old age if we're taking as much radiation as I suspect. We might have fifteen, twenty years, then slow and ugly deaths — and that also matches the fossil record. As far as we can tell, nobody grew old in the distant past. Some of us will also surely develop cataracts before then, and what kind of life will it be, fighting for safety, scratching for food?

Why do I bother? Jan would say because I'm a control freak, won't let even the sun tell me what to do. I had to laugh at that but my voice sounded like a tortured ghost, screeching and echoing all through the building.

Wolsinger hung himself in the stairwell, triple-cinched a tough extension cord and then jumped. Maybe Blair did something, too. Mom ate a bottle of pills and I hated her for it. The doctors said she had a good chance but she didn't want to lose her hair, lose her dignity, suffer through the cure.

I hated Jan for quitting, too.

Hated my father. He also quit in his own way, quit before I was fifteen. It seemed like he put more energy into his stupid basketball games than he gave his own son, football, baseball. He could rattle off a million team statistics and scores but never remembered any of the things I cared about, things that were real and useful.

The EM cone will work, I'm sure of it. And if I do only have fifteen years, at least that's an eternity compared to a life span of days. Life spans. Just thinking about it makes me feel schizophrenic. I'm so tired.

~ ~ ~

More interrupts, two weeks' worth of beard but the moon's in the same phase as when I last recorded it, still waxing full. Madness. Clearly it's waxing again. It's been twenty-eight days and this time I'm going to write before shaving.

Self-awareness came back in jolts and stabs, blurred vision, some dizziness, as if my brain were a rusty engine. The burst of fear-adrenaline squeezing through my heart and limbs probably helped clear my head. I was sitting with a woman in the nest of blankets by the water tanks, a tangy flavor in my mouth and tough, half-eaten roots in my hand.

It was the rancher's daughter. I'll call her Bonita. Apparently about a month ago I shot at her as she threatened me with some kind of gardening tool, but I didn't know that as we sat there staring at each other. I recognized her from long-term memories but hadn't had a chance to read these notes yet. Bonita couldn't have remembered our confrontation either. Despite that and despite having no language in common, we immediately began to argue. She was understandably shocked, vulnerable. I was apologetic and kept my distance, kept my hands up, palms open, my voice low and comforting.

When she ran, I shouted after her like a puppy.

That desperation shouldn't surprise me. It's been several incarnations since I felt anything soft or good or sweet. Bonita was just as dirty as I was but her sweat smelled clean, like perfume synthesized from the pungent earth. She wore only a pair of shorts that were too big for her. I thought I recognized them as mine. It was an American brand. Her breasts were perfect, smooth and small, works of art. And there was the obvious evidence in our nest that we had made love, more than once.

I think we've been together before. I think that what I assumed was a dream of Jan after the previous interrupt was actually some trace of Bonita. Her or someone else. But why would any of the locals come to me? Because of my decorative coloring? I may be the only black man in a hundred miles.

It would be ironic if Bonita had been drawn to this hilltop by some vague memory of it being important, and that when we met we simply acted on our attraction. Enemies when able to think and speak, lovers when reduced to an animal state.

Enemies. Someone tore down the power line running from the cafeteria and sabotaged the generators. Number six is a total loss but I can salvage its auxiliary tank, though there may not be any point if I can't find more fuel. They crawled under the fence, I think, at the saggy corner. More fucking work.

If I save Bonita she'll love me. Jan did for that same reason. Anyone would.

~ ~ ~

Losing too much time to interrupts. My hair is a great Afro

cloud and the damn moon's not making sense, still waxing. Still! I have to write this down to keep from running in circles when I am lucid. Half insane even then, not sleeping.

So close to beating it.

You've already patched together a computer, it's under the armor, stop tinkering with it.

You need to fine-tune your transmitter. The EM hitting us is bizarre, too short, 170 down to 25nm. Maybe Wolsinger was right.

~ ~ ~

The cone works. I'm under it now. Day Three. I've been trying to build a portable version with the few scraps available. It will be very heavy. The generators sound like they're running OK but there's no way to walk out there and check. My biggest fear is that someone will get through the fence again and damage them, turn them off. The noise they make is a liability. I know we still possess curiosity in the animal state.

When the last interrupt stopped I was with Bonita again, making love, close to peaking. She shut her eyes as if to escape me and I paused, but her rhythm increased, maybe involuntarily. Then I slowed again to tease her. She turned to face me and murmured and groaned. We kissed like teenagers. It was wild and raw, far better than with Jan or anyone else ever. But climax was anticlimactic. Desire faded and awkwardness came over us. I tried to make her stay with words and gestures, tried to show her what I was working on, but she kept shaking her head. She ran.

~ ~ ~

Day Five. I just don't have the gear necessary to build a small-er model, and I never had another power source anyway. I'm going to lower the strength of the broadcast, shrinking the safe area to conserve fuel. I think I can push most of my supplies outside the cone and hook them in as needed.

~ ~ ~

Day Nine. I'm not alone. I can see a clearing and the edge of the lake from here and sometimes the locals come up the hill, but they won't enter the building even if I yell, or pretend to be hurt, or sing...

Bonita smiled at that, staring through the fence at my window and moving as close as possible, but she didn't seem to recognize the doors for what they were. Why not?

Our nest was here in this same room.

Maybe it was me she didn't recognize.

I've been studying them. No one talks but there is simple communication, hand gestures, squawks and grunts of impatience, pleasure, agreement. They cooperate. Fortunately, the previous civilization wiped out most of the predators, it's always warm here and the jungle seems to provide enough nourishment for all — and the trees and brush are also shelter from the worst of the ultraviolet.

I didn't mention that I'd lost weight. The desk belly is long gone, but I wasn't starved during the interrupts. In fact there's some evidence that I gorged myself. Obviously I was getting plenty of exercise. Hunting and gathering? And making love. Physically I may be at my best in ten years.

I'm so restless now.

Yesterday I saw Alex Blair playing a fetch-and-chase game with three others. They laughed like kids.

~ ~ ~

Day Seventeen. It's not ever going to end. Even if I had unlimited food and fuel, I can't stay in here forever. Now that I've finally had a chance to breathe, to think it though, I wonder what I'd hoped to accomplish. Escape to a cave and slowly starve there? Study the interrupt phenomenon and create a set of charts and graphs that nobody will ever see?

My biggest fear isn't that the generators will fail. It's that I'll improve my shelter, jury-rig a more permanent protected area, and sit alone in it as the sun flares forever.

I'd have my memories, but would there be any worth keeping?

If I quit now, I win as much as I lose. Bonita. Friends. I want to be a part of their Eden for as long as we have left.

I'll scar my forearm with a short message, in case there are moments of waking confusion and fear. Then I'm going to unchain this journal from my wrist and destroy the generators. I think Dad would be proud to see me pitch a Coke bottle full of gasoline all the way from here.

END

An excerpt from
Frozen Sky 3: Blindsided

1.

Ben said: "Watch your back!"

Vonnie swung around in her suit, lifting one arm to protect her face. In her other hand, she held a sword. Curved and thick and lined with saw teeth, its blade was a wicked crescent.

The tunnels were silent. She heard dripping water. Darkness surrounded them. Her eyes felt as wide as plates.

"What do you see?" she asked.

"Movement. Four contacts," Ben said.

"No," Ash hissed. "There are more."

The three of them weren't supported by mecha or their allies, which left them vulnerable on their flanks. Radar sims allowed them to map several hundred yards of the catacombs — an erratic maze twisting away in all directions — but the shifting ice and trickling streams created dead spots. The noise affected their seismography.

Volcanic hot springs and gas vents filled this region of the frozen sky. The catacombs sagged into low crawl spaces or melted apart in steaming caverns. The ice was pocked with holes.

Now some of those gaps moved as if giving birth. Round muscular forms dropped onto the tunnel floor.

Suddenly there were twelve sunfish on the ice.

Screeching, piping, they writhed their many arms. Most of them were savage males. Their song was hungry and eager, and the few matriarchs did nothing to calm them. The matriarchs' sonar cries were possessive. Worse, this was a poor tribe. Four males and a matriarch showed red fungal infections on their waxy skin. Too many were undersized and thin.

"Oh shit," Ben said.

Vonnie nodded grimly and hefted her sword in both hands. "Get ready to fight."

New sunfish always seemed to have heard of the Earth crews who'd landed on Europa. The tribes could sing to each other through several kilometers of ice, and the ESA biologists thought they often sent runners to carry warnings... but the tribes who hadn't personally dealt with human beings rarely understood the power of lasers or projectile guns, not until they'd been shot.

Vonnie's blade was meant as a deterrent. New sunfish faltered at the obvious cutting edges of medieval weapons. All of the tribes revered metal.

"Don't move!" Vonnie yelled, using her helmet to broadcast her real voice as well as its equivalent in their high-pitched sonar. —*We see you! Don't move!*

—*Danger! Attack!* the males shrieked.

—*There is no danger*, Vonnie cried. —*We're only here for a friend. We are searching for him.*

—*Attack! Attack!*

—*Don't make us hurt you!* she cried.

She kept her elbow close to Ben, covering her side and his. Behind them, Ash touched Vonnie's shoulder, establishing contact even if their heads-up displays placed them within centimeters of each other. A display wasn't as reassuring as a friend's hand.

Ash's voice was rigid with fear. "They're boxing us," she said. "Four ahead, two left, six right."

Vonnie spoke in a reassuring tone. "We can talk to them. We'll make them listen." She gave her AIs a pre-arranged command. "Combat menu, Samurai One," she said.

Their scout suits took over. Two hundred and twenty kilos of armor, computers and ordnance, each suit was capable of moving the human inside it like a person inside a robot.

Unassisted, no human being would have been able to swing their heavy weapons... but in their suits, they were giants. Working through a carefully orchestrated show of force, they danced with the menacing grace of ancient Japanese warriors. Their blades overlapped in a spinning, high-speed pattern.

Before they'd entered the catacombs, Ben and Ash had grabbed battle staffs with axe heads on either end, the better to defend themselves from front and behind. Vonnie preferred her sword. She'd practiced with the long scimitar for hours, and, not coincidentally, its saw teeth resembled the stubby spikes on a sunfish's topside.

Despite their knack for exquisitely subtle nuances in speech and body language, the sunfish were literal creatures. They liked clear connections. The teeth on her blade were a message that even with her height and bulk, she needed defenses, too.

The males shrieked at her, measuring her group with a torrent of sonar calls. —*Food! The intruders are food!* they screamed.

—*Stop! Listen to us!* Maintaining a triangular formation, Vonnie and Ash and Ben advanced on the tribe. —*We will destroy you if you attack!* she cried. —*We are invulnerable and you are small.*

We carry steel.

—*Your name? Your name?* the sunfish called.

Vonnie frowned at the question, and Ash said what she was thinking. "They should know who we are," Ash whispered.

The three of them were 13.4 klicks from their base, well inside the established boundaries of the territory they'd claimed. Their scouts and mecha ranged as far as twenty klicks. They'd placed markers everywhere.

"Cancel one," Vonnie said, stopping the *Samurai* program. It ended with their suits gathered in a confident pose. Vonnie knelt at their center like a matriarch as Ben and Ash stood over her, weapons out. —*We are Ghost Clan Thirty!* she cried.

—*Your name? Your name?* the sunfish called again.

—*We are Thirty!*

The sunfish hadn't declared their own identifiers, which was strange. Were they testing her? Or had their group intelligence been lowered by the predominance of savage males? Vonnie couldn't believe they'd traveled from so far away that they hadn't learned of the new, wealthy, dominant "Ghost Clan" who ruled Europa's southern pole.

She also didn't understand their stubborn repetition, which led her back to one inescapable truth.

Walking into the ice was a death trap.

It's the same damned fight every time, she thought. *Detect, ambush, identify, provoke.*

During the past months, Earth agencies had encountered more than a dozen tribes in addition to a few loners and rogue pairs. Each meeting had begun with violence.

The two males on her left shifted closer. Alarm bars filled her display.

"Here they come!" Ben said.

Vonnie grabbed him. "Wait. Check your display. They're only maneuvering so they can cross their sonar with the six males on our right."

"They're going to jump."

"I'll stop them if they do."

Ben nodded slowly, clutching his axe. Like most of the ESA crew, he mourned the sunfish they'd lost, but he had yet to bend his heart around the fact that killing some of the natives was necessary to save their race.

Vonnie had struggled with that lesson herself. Finally she'd decided to hold onto her guilt like an invisible wound. The horror and fascination she felt toward the sunfish were impossible to separate. She admired so much about them.

Emulating their best traits, she'd also developed an extreme sense of paranoia. Sometimes it let her predict the future. That spooky feeling heightened her composure while Ash's voice tightened in anxiety.

"Why don't they know us?" Ash hissed.

"They do," Vonnie said. "It's a trick. I think more of them are in the catacombs above us."

Ash gaped at her. "What?"

"All systems up. Link to me."

"Oh shit," Ben said as he synchronized his gear block and his tool sets with Vonnie's suit. Ash did the same.

They had ventured beneath the surface with a minimum of active hardware, using radar and nothing else. Spotlights were like torches in the bitter cold. Sonar pulses carried an equal risk. Any disturbance brought predators, including the tribes. The weight and noise of their suits had probably attracted these sunfish, so Vonnie considered herself responsible for whatever happened next. Blood or peace?

"Burn 'em," she said.

Their suits activated every external component. The ice blazed. Her sword gleamed in the light. Unseen, their infrared and sonar exploded outward like a shockwave.

The sunfish recoiled, screaming.

—*WE ARE GHOST CLAN THIRTY!* Vonnie roared. She opened her posture with her sword in one hand and her welding laser on her other wrist. Then she swung away from Ben and her laser flared, slashing into the wall.

A quarter-ton of ice crumbled at her feet.

—*Magma! Quakes! Magma! Run!* a matriarch shrieked, pushing two of the males behind her. Apparently she equated Vonnie's laser with flowing lava.

Vonnie also heard more distant cries. The sunfish hidden overhead had reacted to the terror and astonishment of their kin by promising help... and in doing so, they revealed their positions. There would be no surprise attack, but they were coming quickly.

Her sensors estimated there were twelve of them. The tribe was about to double in size. Would more warriors convince them that they could defeat three people in armor?

Ash and Ben added to Vonnie's roar, their suits mimicking hers exactly as she yelled: —*We can destroy you or we can be allies! We have great strength, but we need workers and guides! We are rebuilding the empire!*

Even as she offered them a treaty, she pinned the nearest

males in her spotlight.

The males cringed. They looked like albino shadows on the ice. Sunfish had no eyes, but they were heat sensitive. Ben also thought they possessed crude photo receptors among the thousands of pedicellaria and tube feet that lined their undersides.

—*Fire!* they screamed. —*Crush it!*

Like a targeting array, they were providing coordinates to their kin. Overhead, the ice vibrated as the hidden sunfish scurried and dug.

Ben looked up.

"Move with me," Vonnie said as she paced closer to the matriarchs. If the sunfish dropped a hunk of ice like a flyswatter, she didn't want to be underneath it.

The matriarchs retreated from her. They argued with the savage males. —*Run! Run!*

—*Crush it! Bury it!* the males screamed.

"Lights off, lasers down," Vonnie said. Their suits complied. Darkness returned as she cried: —*Feel the cold! We control these fires, and our strength can be yours. Join us. Our empire includes many sunfish.*

The matriarchs hesitated. Quivering, they strained forward among the shrieking males. Two of them lifted four arms to expose their tube feet. Tasting the air, listening, they studied Von with the intensity of blind children sifting through a million elusive details.

She knew they could read her tension. They heard her pumping heart and her shallow breaths. They couldn't smell her inside her suit, but she didn't doubt they could discern every clue in her body language as she produced sweat and adrenaline. She tried to master her nerves. At her best, she could project certainty and resolve.

The males continued to scream, disrupting the subtle exchange between Vonnie and the matriarchs.

—*Tell your tribemates above us not to attack*, she warned them. —*We know where they are. If you force us, we will kill you all. Let us help you instead.*

—*Why? Why?* the matriarchs called.

—*We need workers and guides. Join us. We have safe homes. We have limitless food.*

The matriarchs piped among themselves. Their tone was bewildered. It was desperate and yearning. They used their song to quiet the agitated males.

"I think the noise above us stopped," Ben said as Ash blurted in a shaky voice, "I am never coming down here again."

Vonnie didn't have time to comfort Ashley. The matriarchs were considering her offer! She needed to persuade them, so, like a sunfish, she boasted of her tribe's potency once more.

—*We are Ghost Clan Thirty!* she cried.

At last, the matriarchs answered with their own name. —*We are Top Clan Two-Six!*

The combination of low numbers meant they were the dregs of their race, outcasts condemned to the desolate, poisoned sections at the top of the ice. Possibly they were homeless nomads. That was why they'd ignored the markers.

Starving and weak, they'd assumed they were unworthy of an alliance. They must have planned to steal or ambush.

But I got through to them. I scared them enough to listen, she thought. *Now we can nurse them back to health, teach them, help them. We...*

The ceiling collapsed.

Two tons of ice hit the floor where Vonnie had been standing with her teammates. The wind blasted them first. Shrapnel clattered off their suits. Ash staggered in the onslaught and Ben sank to one knee, banging his arm against Vonnie's leg.

There were sunfish in the avalanche. A twitching male fell out of the pile, squashed and bleeding.

—*We are Two-Six!* the matriarchs screamed.

—*Please! No!* Vonnie yelled. But to their kind, begging was taunting. If there had been any chance of changing their minds, she'd ruined it by speaking like she was dealing with people.

The sunfish launched themselves into the air, a swarm of tough-skinned bodies and arms. All twelve acted as one. Some bounced into the wall. Others shoved each other in mid-air to alter their trajectories, careening up or down... spinning off the broken ceiling or the floor... and they converged on the astronauts as a single unit.

Vonnie's radar showed another swarm from behind. Eleven sunfish jumped clear of the avalanche or poured through the gap overhead. She heard Ash shout before the breath was knocked out of her.

Then the matriarchs slapped aside Vonnie's blade. They clawed at her helmet, ripping at her face and neck...

About The Author

Jeff Carlson is the international bestselling author of *Plague Year, Interrupt, Long Eyes,* and *The Frozen Sky.* To date, his work has been translated into sixteen languages world-wide. He is currently at work on a new thriller novel.

Readers can find free fiction, videos, contests and more on his website at **www.jverse.com** including a special Europa-themed photo gallery including images from the *Voyager 1, Galileo,* and *Cassini* probes.

Jeff welcomes email at **jeff@jverse.com**. He can also be found on Facebook and Twitter at **www.Facebook.com/PlagueYear** and **@authorjcarlson**.

Reader reviews on Amazon, Goodreads, and elsewhere are always appreciated.

www.ingramcontent.com/pod-product-compliance
Lightning Source LLC
Chambersburg PA
CBHW060145130626
46556CB00006B/2503